Monogamy Twist

Nancy Jardine

Ocelot Press

Find Nancy Jardine online:
http://www.nancyjardineauthor.com/
Nancy Jardine on Facebook:
https://www.facebook.com/NancyJardinewrites
Follow Nancy Jardine's blog:
https://nancyjardine.blogspot.com/
Follow Nancy on Twitter: @nansjar

Nancy loves to hear from her readers and can be contacted at nan_jar@btinternet.com or via her blog and website.

About the Author

Nancy Jardine lives in the fabulous castle country of Aberdeenshire, Scotland. There are thousands of years of history on her doorstep: fabulous places to visit for research or just for fun, making her interest in all historical periods unlikely to wane. Since retiring from teaching in 2011, she has published work across different sub-genres of fiction. Some contemporary writing reflects her love of ancestry as in *Topaz Eyes* and *Monogamy Twist*. Investigating her ancestral tree is an intermittent hobby which will be revved up when she embarks on the family saga she has on the drawing board.

Her historical fiction *Celtic Fervour Saga Series,* set in northern Roman Britain A. D. 71-84 (north England and Scotland), brings her Late Iron Age Garrigill Clan to life as they battle with the dominance of the invading Roman legions of General Agricola.

The Taexali Game is a time travel historical adventure set in A.D. 210 when Ancient Roman Emperor Severus invades Taexali territory (Aberdeenshire). This is intended for a wide audience from early teens through adult.

Her contemporary romantic mysteries *Take Me Now, Topaz Eyes* and *Monogamy Twist* feature superb world-wide locations. Nancy has been to most of the places in her mystery novels and she challenges her readers to decide which ones, if any, she has NOT yet visited!

When not researching or engaged in various writing tasks, Nancy is a fair-weather gardener and a regular minder of her young grandchildren, all of which keeps her active and highly entertained. As a member of an Aberdeenshire Crafters group, she regularly visits local venues where signed paperback versions of her novels are available for purchase. This direct contact is an excellent way to gain bookings for author presentations which she delivers across Aberdeenshire, tailor made for each group she visits. Some prefer information about her writing life and her novels; while others are hungry for a taste of the ancient historical aspects of their local environment.

Nancy is a member of the Historical Novel Society; the Romantic Novelists Association; the Scottish Association of Writers, the Federation of Writers Scotland, and the Alliance of Independent Authors.

Dedication

The plot for this novel might not have occurred to me if I hadn't been watching the current Charles Dickens serial on TV whilst doing ancestry research on my own family tree. I therefore give my thanks to Charles Dickens, an author whose novels I have great pleasure in re-reading.

My husband is fabulous at feeding me regular super-special meals, and cups of tea and coffee, as I write – and earns my eternal gratitude and love!

Acknowledgements

This new edition has merited only a few changes, the last editor (Kelly May Illingworth) having done a super job.

I give hearty thanks to my fellow authors at Ocelot Press for their continued and incredibly encouraging support during the re-publishing processes and for their unstinting help throughout all the marketing and promotional support after publication.

Monogamy Twist

Chapter One

"Come on, Amelia."

Luke Salieri's curled fist thumped repetitively at the wood.

"Do you reckon I'm such a sucker? Even if I am talking to an effing ghost?"

A response wasn't reasonable because he was talking to a damp wall-covering that oozed around under his warm skin. It was unable to reply to him, just like Amelia Greywood couldn't either, because she'd been dead the best part of two weeks.

"Your conditions are a bloody insult."

Striding off to yet another room, he let off even more steam. The bedroom was brimful of contents as though the room was still lived in, yet no-one had inhabited it for a long time, not even Amelia's ghost. The house wasn't the least bit spooky, but if talking to her damned spirit would conjure her up it would be worth it.

Just to have his many questions answered.

What the Dickens was he going to do about this property?

"Why did you choose me, Amelia?"

He loathed indecision, avoided anything that made him feel vulnerable, but this was like playing some game with pieces missing, knowing his opponent had a full deck, and that only by resorting to some kind of dishonesty would he gain success.

Yet honesty was always Luke's middle name. He was straight in business and candid to a fault in his personal life. Which often annoyed past girlfriends, though right that moment it was Amelia who was the one pissing him off.

He could afford to renovate the dilapidated property, but the rest of her conditions were an antiquated, potentially deceitful nightmare.

Temper barely leashed he confronted the elusive spectre, wishing he could conjure up her image. He couldn't though, because he'd never met the blasted woman.

"So, tell me, Amelia. Where did you dredge up my name from?"

He swept open a Victorian monstrosity of a wardrobe, the epitome of vivid childish nightmares, not surprised to find it still contained flouncy dresses that were moth-eaten and mouldy.

"Hmm? Did you use a pin on a Trades Directory? I hardly think the internet was quite your style. Unless you were an astute silver surfer?"

That notion made him groan. Could Amelia have surfed the web to find the biggest dupe?

Picked for his professional expertise was the only thing that made any sense, the only thing that gave the whole ridiculous scenario any credibility.

He strode to the nearest window to get the smell of camphor-balls out of his nostrils. The tall sash casements were clad with distressed claret brocade drapes, so distressed the colour had sun-faded to a pale blush wine. Pushing aside more cobwebs than material, he flicked the catch and yanked the window open, a shard of deteriorated wood slicing his index finger.

"Shit!"

Curses garbled as he sucked off dripping blood and teased out the substantial splinter with his teeth.

"How could you let a stately old home like this decay so much, Amelia?"

He tried to force the window down again, but it refused to budge, his frustrated grunts disturbed by some wildly frenetic barking.

"What the..." His part-question fogged the windowpane. The beast making the racket was a whirling dervish frolicking over the rough grass.

He grinned, the whimsical interruption lifting his tension.

"Thor. Get back here now!"

The peremptory command came from a woman who was exiting the woods bordering the lawn. Luke smiled again as the excited Irish wolfhound completely ignored its owner, instead bounding up to the dilapidated flagstones of what had once been an impressive terrace way down below him. He considered ignoring his dilemma as well; considered making a similar swift bounce-away.

From his third level vantage point, the young woman recaptured his attention as she ploughed across the overgrown lawn grass. Her husky voice was firm.

"You went off again far too quickly, you disobedient pup."

Pup? The beast was enormous. Luke's focus zoomed in on the woman as she capered back from the animal's attentions. Her lava black hair settled around her chin as she came to a gradual halt and gathered the squirming beast close to her. The dog's tongue lapped out to lick her face, revealing the ungainly quivering of body hair as the long forelegs stretched up onto her shoulders. He watched her almost overbalance under the onslaught of adoration from the dog. She was a tiny little woman, and Thor was one very big canine.

"Get down, Thor!"

The melodious chime of her laughter imprinted itself somewhere inside him as she thrust the hound down to ground level.

"You're not a little pup any more."

Thor? That was a good name for such a powerful beast, he thought, watching her rub the dog's underside. Scratching below his own belly, he adjusted his stance at the window.

His imagination surged, the heat of the sun blasting in the window.

"Who are you?" His question misted the filthy pane, the little pixie below making quite an impact. "A woodland elf?" Well, she had materialized out of the woods and he presently felt he was in some nightmarish fairy tale. His harsh laugh echoed around him in the empty room. Was his fatigue so bad he was hallucinating? An ironic burst peeled out again, loud enough to make the dog's ears perk up.

Warf. Warf.

There was no quiet barking from this particular canine, its exuberance boisterous and excited as it capered way down below the window.

"Come on. Time to go, Thor."

Who was the woman? He watched as she ushered the animal back to the woods. What was she doing in the grounds of Greywood Hall, seemingly so familiar with them? Realising he wanted answers to those questions, Luke erupted into the corridor taking the treads on the internal central staircase two at a time, trusting they'd not collapse under his pounding feet as he hurried outside.

There was no sign of her as he scanned the gardens.

***

Rhia was inside the tree cover when Thor's ears pricked up.

"What is it?" she coaxed, turning back to check. "What are you hearing, boy?"

It wasn't the first time she'd had to prevent her dog from chasing scuttling bunnies on the scraggy lawn.

Not this time. It was no animal Thor heard through the protective shadow of the trees. Someone stood beside the right hand forestair. Where the hell had he appeared from? Something akin to jealousy jolted through her. In all the months she'd been coming into the garden with Thor, she'd never ever seen anyone around. She'd become so used to using the deserted woods and garden for their walks that she'd come to think of this beautiful, though sadly neglected, place as her own. It was upsetting to see someone else here – looking furtive and up to no good.

Bristling with righteous indignation, she tracked the figure peering through every window the man encountered as he rounded the front of the house and made his way along the side wall. Lurking behind a large oak near the edge of the woods her breath hitched, a feeling of alarm pricking her senses, yet curiosity overrode any danger. She wasn't the bravest woman on the planet, yet she was no coward and frankly, she was interested in his stealthy intentions.

"Quiet, Thor." She clutched both his collar and his long pelt, willing his absolute obedience. Sneaking along the fringes of the wood to the walled garden, she approached the house without being visible on the front grass. She might want to know what the stranger was doing, but she wasn't prepared to alert him to her presence. Thor padded beside her as she crept along the cracked paving, quelling the flutter of dangerous exhilaration.

He was a big strapping guy. Dark hair curled at his nape, long enough to touch the neck of his shirt, the hair above it thick and inclined to wave. His soft polo shirt pulled across his powerful shoulders when he stretched up as high as he could reach, blanking out each window. What was he doing? Her focus shifted lower as he moved to the next window: neat jeans tapering over strong, long legs.

"Sexy devil," she whispered to the sky.

Just short of the kitchen door, the man placed his hands on the sill of a narrow window before disappearing, having agilely vaulted inside. Why the heck was he trying all the other windows if he knew that particular one was open?

"The bloody…" Her voice hiked a fraction before she adjusted her volume. "…cheek of him."

The man was breaking and entering. Once more, resentment strummed her nerve ends.

Her breath hitched when his head popped out of the window, her eyes not wanting to believe what she'd glimpsed. He couldn't possibly be that good-looking? Squeezing her eyes shut, she blocked out his image. It was just her luck that she should find the man a stunner.

She faced her dilemma because she was going to have to turn him in to the police.

Once in the safety of the woods, she pulled out her mobile phone. Motioning Thor to remain close to heel, the almost surreal conversation which followed was too confusing for words.

"Yes, I'm safe here in the woods," she reassured the operator. "I'm sure the intruder hasn't a clue that I'm here."

She winced when she had to give her best description of the man, giving as practical a resume as possible, relieved that the operator couldn't see the heat that burned her cheeks. General questions about Greywood Hall were followed by probing inquiries about her own presence there, the implications of which were Just a little bit disturbing.

"Yes, we do. My dog and I squeeze through a little gap in the boundary wall so that he can exercise in the woods, rather than on the lane."

The operator's voice was disheartening. "Miss Ashton, are you confirming that without the owner's permission you regularly exercise your dog on this property?"

"I've told you. I'm the nearest neighbour to Greywood Hall and…" The line beeped, then nothing. As she stared at her dead phone, something about those last questions made her feel uncomfortable. "Well, that was just bloody dandy. I guess they're not interested in lawbreakers today."

Her concern clearly unwanted, she ordered Thor back to heel and continued on her afternoon walk.

A short while later, on approaching the main drive to Greywood Hall, Rhia was stunned when she noticed that someone had forced the ancient padlock. It dangled from its huge chain, the rusty gates wide open. It hadn't been like that earlier when she had passed by.

It was only when Thor nudged her back onto the short embankment she realised that the yellow and blue checks on the white vehicle indicated a police patrol car was slowing down to a halt beside her, the front passenger window partially open.

"Excuse me, miss? Would you be Rhia Ashton of Border Cottage?"

"Yes." She bent towards the officer to reply. "That would be me."

"You recently made an emergency call?"

"I…Yes. I did."

It was too late to wish that she hadn't donned the Neighbourhood Watch cap.

A torrent of irate words blasted out from the back of the car, freezing her to her very marrow. It sounded like Italian and devastating, since the malice ridden tirade was directed straight at her. She knew holiday phrases like please and thank you, and not much else, though was positive some of the words coming at her wouldn't be found in an ordinary dictionary. She reeled away from the still closed back window as the intruder changed to just as loud English.

"This is absolute nonsense. You're the one who informed the police?"

Rhia was transfixed for the handsome face she'd glimpsed earlier wasn't quite so appealing, now. What the hell had made her think he was good looking? Thor growled alongside her, baring his teeth as he propped his paws up against the door, his mass a defensive bulwark.

"I watched you down there on the lawn with that huge apology for a dog, and you have the nerve to call the police about me."

The man was livid. She was in no doubt he was incensed that she'd had the effrontery to call the police about him.

"Be quiet please, sir!"

The constable's authoritative tone was ignored; the intruder's mixture of mumbled Italian and English continuing to berate her. He crept forward in his seat forcing her to shrink back from the car, his piercing green eyes malevolent.

Tracking his sturdy fingers as they reached forward to grasp the sides of the headrest behind the uniformed officer, she fantasized them grasping themselves around her neck, stifling the life out of her. The burglar was so full of suppressed fury.

"Sit back please, sir, and let us deal with this matter."

Rhia's manic vision shattered, the constable's stern voice jolting her back to the present as the intruder slunk back under the officer's unyielding glare.

"We'll need you to accompany us to the police station, Miss Ashton. We have a few matters to sort out about Greywood Hall, but please take the hound home first."

She managed a dumb nod, aware that the officer had raised the car window to almost the top the minute Thor's paws had touched the side of the vehicle. Grabbing the dog's long pelt, she stumbled off the verge on rickety legs and lurched along the short distance to her cottage. The low grumble of the police vehicle slithered down her back as it tailed her home. They were going to ask her all sorts of questions about why she was on the premises. Guilt now gripped her in a vice because breaking some kind of law was a dead cert.

Having secured Thor in the fenced off dog run in her back garden, she returned to the squad car as requested.

"Thank you for that, Miss Ashton." The constable's tone was brisk, though there was no anger in it as he got out of the vehicle to open the back door for her. "If you wouldn't mind getting in please, then we can be off."

Chapter Two

"You're expecting me to get into the back of the car with him?"

Luke's anger dissipated into a little quirk of satisfaction. It didn't take much effort to read into the little pixie's expression that she was thoroughly dismayed by the request.

"Come along, Miss Ashton." The constable was firm. "We need to talk to you both back at the police station, but it will take a while before another vehicle can be put at our disposal for you to be transported separately."

Rhia Ashton was still not placated, her panic evident in the wide brown eyes that were too scared to focus on anyone. The officer's tone lightened a little and became cajoling. Luke suppressed a snarl at the new strategy.

"Let's get on and sort out this little misunderstanding." The officer's smile was forced as he corralled her into the car. "We've discussed this with Mr. Salieri, and we know you'll be safe in the back, so don't you worry now."

Her expression indicated she didn't think much of the explanation. Did she think he was any happier as she was poured in beside him?

He was infuriated that she had informed the police about him. He understood the reticence of the police officers to accept him at face value, acknowledging that he didn't at that moment look in the least like the head of his successful construction business.

Though it was demeaning, being conducted to the local police station was the quickest and most expedient way they could verify, without doubt, the details about his potential ownership of Greywood Hall. He knew that, but he didn't have to like it.

Being escorted in a police car didn't sit at all well with him – with or without Miss Ashton.

She scuttled like a little mouse beside him, cowering into as tiny a space as possible on the far side of the bench seat. What the devil did she think he was going to do to her? His angry Italian muttering accompanied frustrated thrusts of his fingers through his thick dark hair, expecting the locks to stay off his forehead. He was in a squad car with two police officers in the front. Did she think he was stupid enough to assault her? Though at that moment, he did feel like he could happily wring her neck and ignore the fact that it was a tasty little morsel. How could the woman look so good and be so dense at the same time? First she thought he was a burglar? Now, some perverted attacker?

He might want to pounce on her, though not quite the way she was thinking from the scowls she was giving him. Deep brown eyes with tiny little flecks of grey looked justifiably upset, perversely cheering him. Crossing his arms to keep temptation at bay he forced his features to relax. He smiled at her, a calculating scheming smile because she didn't know what she was in for – this little imp of the woods.

"Soon be at the station, Mr. Salieri," the constable in front informed him breaking into his train of thought. "We'll have this little misunderstanding sorted out soon enough."

Luke continued to stare at Rhia Ashton. A short little name. It really suited her. Rhia had a nice tinkling sound, though admiring her name and super-tempting physical attributes was one thing – thinking about her damned interfering behaviour was quite another. What had the stupid woman done? Poking her dinky nose into his business?

Peering at his watch, he noted how long it had been since he'd had to acquiesce with the police officers and get into their vehicle. He'd frittered away enough hours already and was squandering more in order to extricate himself from this inadvertent muddle.

"This is a waste of my damned time!" His reproach came through grated teeth as she twitched next to him, her neck muscles straining to keep herself facing forwards.

"What the hell did you think you were doing?" His low pitch demanded a response, and he didn't care one iota if he was upsetting her because she'd just caused him no end of hassle.

"They thought I was a burglar." He moved closer. "What made you think I was breaking and entering the property?"

He paused for a reply that didn't come; his intent gaze focused on her before accepting his insistent pressure wasn't working. The woman was refusing to even make eye contact with him never mind buttoning her little lips. It was time to change tack. He opted for more subtle persuasion.

"Tell me, Rhia. Nice name, by the way." He made sure his tone softened to a mesmerising murmur. "I deserve to know why." The change of pitch worked a treat when she whipped round towards him.

"You are a burglar! I saw you climbing in a window that you'd forced open. Before that I watched you try all the downstairs windows."

Luke processed her words his eyebrows drawing together in a slight frown. "That makes me a burglar?" He moved back from her, his remaining irritation turned to pure frustration. "You don't have an effing clue!" His determined whispers hit the mark when her cheeks flushed, but she refused to speak again. Regardless of his immense effort to sound more rational, her little pointed chin stuck up into the air.

He stopped whispering though kept staring, cataloguing every single one of her features, and then shifted uncomfortably. What kind of moron got aroused – in a police car – eyeing up an interfering woman who'd just had him arrested? His bold stares paid off, though, when her eyes clashed with his for a fraction of a second before she dropped her gaze.

A grin spread across his face that he didn't even attempt to stifle. She blushed like a lantern flare. A small smile of sheer satisfaction curled his lips. Sliding down on the seat, he lounged and folded his arms across his chest. He rested his head on the seat back and closed his eyes, the lack of sleep catching up.

He chuckled again.

It had been a long time since he'd been near a woman who could colour up like that.

Moments later he hurtled across the seat, his seatbelt stretching to its limit as the car swerved round an almost right-angled bend. He knew he should avoid some of the contact made, but it was just too fortuitous. His cheek finding an appetizing cushion on impact was way too appealing. He squashed any instinct to halt his sideward lurch and found her soft breast.

"Get off me, you big oaf!"

From such an awkward, luscious position Luke raised his eyes. He didn't even want to attempt to wipe the entertainment from his gaze, though her indignant command deserved some response. Right beside his cheek her fresh-meadow smell might have been a laundry product or her unique fragrance – he didn't care – it filled his nostrils.

How could he not nuzzle a little as he unfurled his crossed arms? The temptation was far too much to deny as he used her quivering leg muscle as a prop to push himself upright, her gasp at his effrontery the most entertaining thing he'd experienced in ages.

A laugh bellowed from the driver.

"I should have warned you about that corner. Mr. Salieri."

The shock on the woman's face again indicated a near combustion. He pulled his grin back into order.

"Sorry."

His apology, it seemed, wasn't quite sincere enough because she remained flustered, her eyes furious, but he was on a roll. He wanted to get to know this little woman a bit better.

His none-too-subtle wink seemed to be the icing on the cake.

"Stop that right now!"

Amusement at her husky command wasn't appreciated: Rhia Ashton turned her back on him, peering out of the window – probably at nothing.

He settled back into his end of the seat, hoping the journey wouldn't last much longer. He closed his eyes and slid into a delicious daydream, drifting to horizontal surfaces and lots of skin…some of it blushing rosily, and smelling delightfully. At first he let the visions flow until, with a few savage Italian curses, he willed his thoughts elsewhere.

Greywood Hall. What the hell was he going to do about that?

He needed a woman right enough, and soon.

***

Some time later Rhia was the sole occupant of a tiny interview room where she'd been dumped after a brief identification process and some lengthy questions about her call to the emergency services operator. She wondered why they had just left her stewing. Was this part of normal procedure?

She hadn't a clue since she'd never been in a police station before and didn't know what kind of crime they thought she had committed.

Dog fouling?

They could definitely get her on that one. She'd allowed that repeatedly; how was she to stop Thor from doing a bit of business in the wood? Sometimes it happened on the lane, her pooper-scooper always at the ready – though in the wood? That was a different matter entirely. Could they charge her for being on private property? Holy shit! That one was a definite yes.

Unfortunately, the solitude gave her far too much time to reflect on the bizarre happenings of the afternoon. In a very opposing way, it had been the most exciting day and also the most perplexing one she'd had in years. Another shudder rippled down her back, this time a physical re-creation of her earlier feelings. In the rear seat of the patrol car, her responses to the gorgeous, but crooked, Mr. Salieri had been a volatile mixture of stimulation and dread.

When he'd stopped his relentless questioning, after she'd continued to ignore him, the embarrassing deathly silence in the back seat had continued the rest of the way to the police station, interspersed by the low murmurs of the officers and by the incomprehensible crackle of the police radio. Silence almost the rest of the way, except when the burglar's face had slammed into her boobs. He hadn't even acknowledged her shocked outburst at the driver's words.

He'd merited the apology? She didn't think so. If she hadn't already been so fired up, the injustice of it would have made her blood roil.

The physical contact made by the collision had been so annoyingly arousing. The stranger's cheek had twitched against her, and the little olive flecks in his grass green eyes had intensified as he'd glanced up at her face, so close she could see the new stubble on his cheeks and the soft skin of his lips. Close enough to smell the remnants of a woodsy fragrance, or maybe that had just been his naturally enticing male scent? Didn't matter. It had hit her senses like a sledgehammer even more powerfully than his cheek on her flesh.

He'd been playing her like a violin; she knew it yet hadn't been able to stop it.

She didn't expect the officer's words when he eventually returned.

"Miss Ashton. Thanks for your cooperation. I'm sorry we've kept you waiting so long. It transpires that we don't need to talk to you any more about your presence at Greywood Hall. We've a patrol car waiting outside to take you home, so if you'll come this way please?"

***

"I've never before thanked anyone for arresting me, but now I definitely will." Luke beamed as he exited the officer's patrol car for the second time that afternoon. "You've actually done me a big favour."

After he clicked his car open, he waved them off. His journey to the police station hadn't been a waste of time after all: in fact, it was the catalyst needed to make him determined to keep Greywood Hall with all its ridiculous restrictions.

Once his status as prospective owner of the estate had been verified, he'd been able to initiate the processes for gaining authorised permits for a variety of local road transport requirements which would be needed for renovations at Greywood Hall. His unscheduled visit had just circumvented some tedious, though always necessary, phone calls and official local authority form filling.

There were just a few minor details to organise. Well, more than a few. His grin was wide with no hint of possible failure tainting it. Climbing inside his car, he whipped out his mobile phone, switched it on and placed a call.

"Hi, Jeremy." Barely drawing breath he reeled off instructions. "Get Braydon Security right away and request immediate details on Rhia Ashton of Border Cottage." Jeremy's quick question was easily answered. "Yes. It's the same postal area as Greywood Hall. I want everything they can find, immediately."

A swift update on his movements that day was followed by a long list of tasks, Luke's PA asking few questions. "No." Luke responded to the last one. "Nothing's wrong with my mobile. I purposely switched it off after our last call while I was assessing the property."

15

"You switched it off?"

Luke grinned at the total disbelief coming from Jeremy, unsurprised by his PA's next statement. "I've dealt with what's been forwarded to me, Luke, though you're going to have some pile to deal with on your own voice-mail now."

A little pause followed. He killed time, his smile widening, since he knew Jeremy wasn't quite done yet.

"Was the place so awful?"

"Big updates on that later," he snorted in response because Jeremy, his PA of five years, always knew when to be diplomatic. "Let's just say some unplanned hitches held me up. I'll likely give a green light on it, but the decision's still a little undecided." Jeremy's professionalism was what he paid well for as the conversation switched straight back to business matters. "Sure, give me the details on that now."

Grabbing a pen from the glove compartment, he lifted a file from the stack on the passenger seat and located the sheets he required. Noting the particulars given, he added the information and fielded numerous questions about other business matters. Then, satisfied with what had just been set up, he finished the call, "By the way Jeremy, don't have a heart attack if my phone is switched off again later this afternoon."

Luke clicked off his phone; his reply to Jeremy's last question evasive. Did something at Greywood Hall require more of his time and attention? Yes, something did, though nothing directly to do with the building itself, like Jeremy had implied.

An hour and a half later, a bundle of other calls accomplished – some made and some received – he felt he was more than ready to take up the challenge of Greywood Hall.

Turning his car, he headed for Border Cottage. What he now knew about Rhia Ashton was ideal; in fact, she might have been tailor made for him to help solve the quandary of Greywood Hall. If he could coerce Miss Ashton to fit in with the plans he'd just made, precious time wouldn't be wasted. The women in his current social sphere were unsuitable for the bizarre requirements imposed by the very dead Amelia Greywood, but Rhia Ashton looked just the thing.

Had it only been a little more than a day since this farcical merry-go-round had started?

His growl filled the car interior as he reviewed the recent events. The previous morning his life had been going according to plan as he journeyed back to London, though the rest of the day hadn't quite panned out anything like he'd intended.

"You've been bequeathed a property in the Yorkshire Dales known as Greywood Hall," his lawyer, John McBride, had stated.

"You have to be joking!" He'd refuted the declaration, though John was a friend as well as a colleague. He wouldn't pull a joke of this magnitude. "I don't know anybody called Amelia Greywood."

"That may be the case Luke, but you are specified, listed as beneficiary of Miss Greywood's will. There's no doubt that the property has been bequeathed to you. There are no further beneficiaries involved as the small monetary gifts to Beechlee Nursing Home staff have already been dispensed with, all in accordance with the will."

"Surely there must have been some relative, or friend, or other poor sod that the property could have been left to?"

"No. Miss Greywood's instructions are unambiguous. You're the main and only remaining beneficiary." John had gone on to spell out the terms of the will in detail so that there would be no misunderstandings.

After pacing around his spacious office for a few stunned minutes, during which time John had maintained a discretely polite silence, he had ceased his tramping. Some very necessary questions had needed further clarification. Bracing his hands on his desk, his questions had rattled out.

"Let me get this straight. The whole property is approximately ninety acres. Ninety acres?" John's nod had encouraged him to continue. "Okay, ninety acres, including the main house, and various outbuildings. Some of the land is currently leased out." His mood had been sceptical. "It will be mine along with the small sum of six thousand, four hundred and twenty four pounds?"

John McBride's expression had wavered from a frozen blank mask, the wince only barely discernible. "You're being obtuse, Luke. I've made it clear that could be the case after one year."

"It could be? In one year? You're also telling me that although my name is indisputably on that will, I can't dispose of it just now as I see fit?" He'd clumped around a bit more as he'd pondered the rest of the unwelcome revelations of the will.

John had cleared his throat. "That's correct. The property will be yours to eventually deal with, as you choose, though only if you use it for a period of at least one calendar year as a personal domicile in cohabitation with your spouse. And…if that period of residence is initiated within one month from today."

"Bloody hell, John. You know I don't have a wife, and I've no intention of getting one any time soon, so I'm not likely to fulfil that little gem, am I?"

John had again cleared his throat before adding, "We've tried to find a way around this term, but it's watertight."

"Probably much more watertight than the property itself I imagine?"

"As to that I couldn't say. My information states that Miss Greywood had been living in Beechlee Nursing Home for twelve years prior to her death and that the property has been locked up during that time."

"Twelve years? Has nobody been there at all?" The concept was incredulous.

"Twice yearly a representative from the local lawyer's office ensured that the property was undisturbed."

"So, to become owner of this estate I have to conjure up a wife to have sex with as my cohabitee. I'll probably also have to fork out a fortune to restore this property to be able to use it as a main domicile living as a happy family with this, as yet fictitious woman." He'd thundered on. "And if I don't meet all of these terms – what happens to this property?"

"The property will eventually revert to the crown after a period of fifty years. During that time nobody at all will be allowed to do anything to repair, maintain or even demolish the property, save what weather and age will do itself."

"By which time a substantial piece of land, not to mention a house of the size you're indicating, will be completely ruined. The waste's unthinkable!" He had paced around his office like a demented tiger, knowing full well John was only the messenger and not the perpetrator of this profligate proposition. "Renovation costs I can handle. You of all people know that, John." He'd spat the last out, thumping a fist on his desk and had then collapsed into his chair. He'd thrust his fingers through his thick dark hair, and forced his voice level to reduce. "Though the other terms are just downright farcical, not to mention archaic. What was the crazy woman thinking?" At that point, he'd exhausted the vocabulary to vent his spleen.

At thirty-three, his life was good; on course for the way he wanted it to be. He handled large properties on a daily basis. He knew how marketable such a sizeable property could be, even in the wildest area of Britain – and the Yorkshire Dales wasn't that. He'd carved a niche for himself over the years buying up properties just like Greywood Hall, renovating and marketing them as corporate residential venues with multiple options for work and leisure pursuits on site. He had solid construction businesses in Australia, and more recently in the UK, and had earned a respected reputation along the way. He could buy a property like this on the open market in a snap and do what the hell he wanted to it.

However, he didn't need a total stranger to bequeath it to him in their will. And he definitely didn't need anybody, alive or dead, to dictate his marital status.

John had again cleared his throat, merely an 'attention-grabbing' strategy. "I have to point out, Luke, that although the will terms might seem archaic to you, it would, I repeat, it would be perfectly legal for you to walk out onto the street right now and marry the first woman you bump into. So long as the woman in question has no legal impediments to the marriage and is in agreement, all you need is a signature on the marriage licence."

"Just a signature? What about the cohabit clause?"

John smiled for the first time. "Luke. The lawyers won't be putting CCTV into your bedroom. You need to have a spouse. You need to live in the same house as her, but that doesn't mean you have to have sex with her."

Luke's swear word was particularly appropriate.

"Time will tell regarding that one." John's grin betrayed his thoughts.

"I want to know everything you can about this ridiculous bequest."

John nodded. "I'll get Braydon Security to do a background check on Amelia Greywood, and see if we can find more about why you're the beneficiary, though I can't promise anything. The local lawyer could shed no information for me when I asked him."

Now, as he drove to Border Cottage, Luke felt maybe he could do something about this ridiculous legacy. Rhia Ashton might possibly be the key – an answer to his prickly problem. His mood enlivened for the first time in hours as he drove along the sun-flashed leafy lanes. His energy levels perked up again, not due to the caffeine fix he'd had from the lousy coffee at the police station, but from the anticipation of speaking again with Rhia Ashton.

The pixie of the woods.

Chapter Three

Gawping at the document spread out in front of her, the words made absolutely no sense. Rhia's usual concentration was shot. The weird dismissal from the police station played out in her head like a continuously repeated refrain. She conceded that her regular forays into the woods at Greywood Hall had been trespassing, and her conscience niggled like a rotting mouth abscess. She detested unresolved issues.

Knowing it didn't make it any easier to get on with her work.

Her vision constantly reran the burglar's dark scowls and persistent questions: her emotions so tangled she'd already snapped three pencils. Chewing her bottom lip, her grunts were extremely unfeminine – wasn't it typical that she felt attracted to a sodding loser yet again?

Fingering aside the document, she headed back to her computer hopeful that she'd have better focus with online researches.

Her life story wasn't going to repeat itself. Her last boyfriend, the serial-sex-cheater of the century, had been cunning enough to conceal that little facet of his personality for months, before a kind acquaintance had spilled the beans on at least five other women he was boinking.

She shuddered at the memory of the boyfriend before that, cringing at her naivety. He, at least as far as she knew, hadn't been screwing loads of other women, but he'd owed money to half of London and hadn't a scooby to pay them back. Especially not all the hard earned cash he'd temporarily borrowed from her – since a permanent job had never seemed to be in his grasp.

Never again.

She wasn't ever again going to be suckered by good-looking, sweet-talking walking disasters. That was why she'd removed herself to rural Yorkshire, to get herself out of their orbit and away from the temptations of London society. In reality, she still had so much debt she couldn't afford to live in London any more.

Thor's agitated barking penetrated the fug she was in. Someone was buzzing her doorbell.

"Piss off!"

Rhia had often been told she was a little woman with a very big hair-trigger. Making nice to visitors, right that moment, held no appeal at all. What she wanted was to wallow in the bewilderment and guilt-driven anxiety that had settled on her like the Sword of Damocles. Unfortunately, her sensitive gut was warning her that those unresolved issues were now about to smack her in the face.

In the backwater where she lived any caller was a rarity, save Gus who was her only regular visitor. It couldn't be him though, since Thor never made a racket when Gus arrived. Frustration screamed in her head. The only way to shut Thor up was to find out who was there. Yanking her heavy front door open, her inhospitable glare was meant to deter.

Good lord!

What the hell was Salieri-the-snooping-burglar doing here on her doorstep? The last person she expected to confront stood right outside. Why wasn't he locked up in a police cell?

"What do you want?"

Knees buckling, Rhia decided she didn't actually want to wait for an answer and shoved the door closed. In a flash, his foot blocked the space, the rest of his large body bending back from the entryway. Short of crushing his toes to bits, and she was very tempted to do just exactly that, she found herself unable to deny him access though she did her best to wedge him out.

"I'm not going to hurt you, I promise. Please believe me," he explained, his hands held up in a gesture of surrender.

Those searching green eyes sought her compliance, though his conciliation was barely discernible over Thor's tumult in the back garden. Processing his dry chuckles, he seemed genuinely amused.

She winced. What a strange man. Who in their right mind would find the combination of Thor's rumpus and such an awkwardly spine-bending position at the door amusing?

"Look, I need to talk to you." His tone softened as he pleaded, "To explain about earlier."

Rhia fought the instinct to get rid of him. He did, after all, look sincere now and though he blocked the door, he wasn't threatening her. With his strength it would be a doddle to push inside, and she'd not be able to prevent it. Her five feet three was no competition for his frame that was well over six feet, built like a tree trunk and likely twice as heavy.

"Would you please call off the demented watchdog and tell him I'm a friend," his dark treacle voice cajoled, seeping around her aggravation.

Gone was the ferocious stranger in the car, gone the drawn brows and black frown. Far better looking than a downright shady character ought to look. She was disgusted at herself because any alarm had drifted off on the wind, a perverted curiosity replacing it since she really did want to know what the hell game this man had been playing along at Greywood Hall.

"You're definitely not my friend!"

"How can you know that? You don't have any inkling about me."

"Who are you, then?" Her grip on the door relaxed as tension seeped out of her taught arm muscles. She'd give him the benefit of the doubt.

"My name's Luke." He eased his foot free, tilting his head a little closer. "Officially Lucca Salieri, though I'm always called Luke."

"I know that bit." Rhia huffed. "But who are you really?"

"I'm not here to hurt you, I promise."

Her fingers remained glued to the still partially opened door, Thor continuing his hullabaloo.

He winced at the horrendous noise, valiantly trying to prevent the creasing up of the flesh over his cheekbones, though he was failing as his irritation at the dog was too difficult to stifle.

"I'd really like to explain what I was doing at Greywood Hall – but can you tell your bloody hound to shut up first so you might hear me?"

She gave a perfunctory nod; her mind made up. "You'd better come in."

All business she opened the door wide, ushering him into the narrow hallway that stretched from front to back of the cottage. The man had put her through enough fluctuations of seesawing emotions already that day so she would let him explain himself, and she had to calm Thor anyway. Relinquishing her hold on the door, she closed it shut and made her way through the small hallway, beckoning him to follow.

"Enough, Thor!" Her command barked out as she opened the back door. "Quit your yowling."

The dog, in full defence mode, advanced towards Luke who'd come outside behind her.

"Sit!" she ordered, afterwards bending down to reassure the dog, stroking his coat from head to tail, deliberately softening her voice. "Thor. I'm fine. It's all right, boy." Thor stopped his barking, his tail thumping around Rhia's legs, still excited though obeying her. "This is Luke," she instructed the dog. "Say hello."

Luke presented his hand for inspection. Thor sniffed around him for a few seconds, accepted the cautious stroking offered then obediently sank to the ground at the man's feet. Rhia grinned at the surreptitious tug Luke made to his polo shirt collar. Maybe showing some relief that Thor had accepted him?

"Good boy." Her delight with Thor's perfect behaviour was evident. "It'll be all right now, he's happy," she explained to Luke, now the one doing the reassuring. "Let's go back inside."

Making sure it didn't escape his notice, she purposely left the back door wide open. In her bright sitting room, he sat on the wooden rocking chair she indicated. Stilling the movement of the rock, he braced his feet firmly on the wooden floor then hung his hands loosely over his knees, his strong fingers open and comfortable on the dark grey denim. Guilt kicked back in with a vengeance as she took the smaller seat opposite him on the other side of the fireplace.

Maintaining eye contact with him was downright impossible so instead she fixed on the decorative logs and vase of dried grasses that filled the grate while she carefully composed her words.

"You wanted to explain?"

"I'd like to clear up this misunderstanding from earlier today."

At her mute nod he continued.

"First of all, I'm not the burglar you suspected." A hint of humour sneaked in, no doubt a deliberate strategy on his part. His mouth twitched, and a tiny smile appeared to soften the contours of his strong jaw line, his gaze comfortingly earnest. "In addition, I assure you I haven't escaped from police custody. They didn't need to keep me down at the police station since I wasn't committing any offence."

Rhia wasn't convinced. "You were trying all the widows, and I saw you climbing into one." Her voice faltered when he grinned, a full-bodied grin that rocked her equilibrium again.

"You're right about that." Contrarily, his nod confirmed her statement as truth as he further explained. "I was checking all the windows, and I did climb inside the one I'd purposely broken into."

"But you…"

"The reason the police didn't book me is because I've just become the new owner." Something between a grimace and a puzzled grin spread across his face, his deprecating gaze making a mockery of what he'd just said. "Well, you could say that I'm almost the new owner of the property."

"You're buying it?" she hazarded. He sounded so unsure, his comment was baffling. At his minutest head shake she added, "It doesn't quite belong to you yet?"

"You're good," he chortled. "Those are excellent questions with no easy answers, Rhia." He sought her confirmation as he continued, "May I call you Rhia?"

She gave a tiny nod of assent. He pointed to a row of paperbacks nearby.

"My almost ownership probably reads like one of those mystery novels on your shelves. You'll need some background to my story, so I'd really appreciate it if you'll listen." His tone encouraged her compliance.

She nodded, resolved to hear him out though she needed a prop, something to fiddle with as she listened to him, so pasting an almost polite smile on her face her inquiry was tentative. "Is this a stiff drink story?"

Heartened by his grin she burbled on, "No brandy I'm afraid, though I've got some white wine chilling in the fridge?"

"The wine sounds excellent but not the answer for me right now. Alcohol would probably knock me comatose since I've been travelling almost non-stop for three days." His smile widened. "A cup of tea would be good, though."

"You drink tea?"

"Hey, I'll have you know my mother brought me up like a good little English boy. Well, at least my nannies did."

Her slight frown and pursed lips must have amused him for he divulged a bit more.

"Tea at four p.m. in the drawing room was an afternoon requirement. I was summoned from the nursery to attend from quite a young age."

The nursery? Rhia's eyebrows almost hit the rafters as her breath halted in her throat. She somehow didn't believe he was talking about a state nursery attached to a primary school like the one she'd attended with around thirty other kids. And the drawing room he was talking about? It didn't sound like her art classroom either.

Lurching up, Luke paced to the window. His amusement dwindling, his next words were acidic as he studied the view outside before he continued. "Sadly, the tea ceremony was in the nature of training the child, presided over by the current nanny, for neither my mother nor my father attended often, even at weekends. They were far too busy building up their respective business empires."

His baffled expression showed some regret at parting with that tiny bit of information.

"Tea's coming up but don't look for any fancy formal procedure from me, Mr. Salieri!"

She headed for the kitchen to rally her thoughts, wondering what the hell she was doing turning her back on him. Who was he? Could he be joking? A very convincing con man? Rhia filled her electric kettle with water and plugged it in; her churning gut telling her he wasn't. If he was genuine, what she did know was that she wasn't in his financial league – not in a million years.

***

Rhia's pragmatic tone somehow cheered Luke. She looked to be a frank woman, exactly what he needed. Sentimentality would be far too messy for what he sought for the coming year.

His glance encompassed the sitting room. Though small, it was cosy with bright accents in cushions and decorative elements, yet there was a practicality about it.

The large oak dining table, which was fully extended below the window, was a work station of sorts. There was a pleasant mish-mash of tidy piles and messy areas, at first glance looking haphazard but on second with some sort of order in mind, all at hand and ready for researching.

Realistic.

Exactly the kind of woman he needed.

He followed her, lounging his large body on the doorframe to the small kitchen. While she assembled mugs, milk, sugar and biscuits from a jar, he continued to explain why he was at Greywood Hall.

"Think Dickensian novel, Rhia. Think really unusual bequests and a strange benefactress, and you're part way there."

As his tale continued, he was conscious of her derision, sensing that she was finding him a tad delusional. That wasn't wrong since he was feeling that way himself. On balance though, when he interpreted her reactions, she was intrigued in a totally silent way that amused him.

She listened while gathering fillings for sandwiches. Salad greens he could do without, though he was pretty partial to stacked layers of roast beef and mustard. His stomach growled in anticipation.

"Yesterday, I was on the last stage of a very long flight back from Brisbane, having spent the last two weeks there on business," he resumed. "Not far out of London, I picked up a message from my London legal team requesting an immediate meeting to discuss matters of a personal nature."

"You're Australian?" Rhia interrupted as the electric kettle clicked off after boiling. "Is that why you have a very unusual accent?"

He chuckled, appreciating her deft movements with the kettle and a ceramic teapot. "It sure is. Australian with Italian inflections, though my English boarding schools were supposed to knock that out of me. They didn't quite erase all traces, much to my father's atypical delight, and my mother's extreme annoyance."

She swirled hot water around the teapot then dunked it in the sink before adding fresh tea to the warmed pot, her glances in his direction alternating between being wary and intrigued.

"Your father's Australian?"

"He was Italian, hence the name Salieri. My mother was Australian, though at times she liked to brag about her eminent distant English forebears. She was snob of the first order, was my mother, and she derided anyone and everyone whose ancestry was in any way suspect – at least in her opinion."

He was surprised to find that he didn't mind filling in snippets of personal information in answer to Rhia's polite questions while she efficiently bustled about in the small space. He needed to tell her sufficient, anyway, to ensure she'd acquiesce to his plans. He needed a level-headed woman.

That she was very easy on the eye was a definite bonus. Clearing his parched throat, he called his errant thoughts to order when he realised their tea tray was ready.

"So let's get back to yesterday." He straightened his six foot four frame, took the loaded tray, and followed her back into the sitting room. Setting it down on the small coffee table she had swept clear of magazines, he paced around the room like a penned up animal.

"Personal legalities are handled by my Australian lawyers, so it was exceptional to be asked for a meeting in London."

Rhia was so transparent in her interest. He hoped that would work in his favour.

"My UK lawyer gave me some astonishing information, yesterday." Circumnavigating the room twice, he positioned himself by the window. He half-sat on the edge of the cluttered dining table and gave the stacked historical papers a cursory glance.

As she approached carrying a mug of tea, not a delicate cup and saucer he was glad to note, her gaze flickered to the car parked outside: his top of the range Ferrari. She looked a little flustered as she relinquished the tea into his hands.

"Sorry," she said sweetly, brushing fingers with him. "I'm all out of lemon today."

He ignored her sarcasm. "No problem. I take tea with milk."

"Help yourself," she indicated the tray, "and to the food, too." Amusement glowed in her liquid brown gaze as she added, "I'm not your servant. You'll get no ceremony here, Mr. Salieri."

Luke strode over to add some milk to his mug, pleased that she had a bit of spunk.

She sipped her tea delicately. He closely watched her reactions to his story, wondering how she'd respond.

"Yesterday, I was informed that I'd been named as the sole beneficiary of the will of Miss Amelia Greywood – a woman I'd never heard of, by the way – and that I'd inherited her property called Greywood Hall." A good slug of his tea slipped down as he let that sink in.

"Earlier you said you were almost the owner, but now you're saying she did leave it to you?"

The bewilderment was evident on her face, her gaze and tones suspicious.

"Both are true." His words were staccato as he prowled the room.

"You're not pleased about it?" Rhia's tone indicated his snippy answer had startled her.

Contrary to her earlier statement about being a servant, she reached for a plate and offered him a sandwich which he devoured in almost one bite. Absently he reached for another, striding around while he chewed, then he picked up a third. He was starved.

"Not particularly," he answered when he'd eventually finished chewing the third sandwich, appreciating them all. It had been hours since he'd eaten anything substantial.

"And you'd never ever heard of Miss Greywood?"

Her fascination about the unfolding story was clear as she delicately ate a sandwich. Good thing too, Luke thought, before they all disappeared off the plate because he was still ravenous.

"Never." He explored the mini-office set up in the corner of the room as he drained his mug before re-filling it from the teapot. She seemed to encourage no formality which greatly heartened him, though he knew his manners lacked some finesse. His gaze strayed to the bookcase groaning with history tomes.

"Did you know Amelia by any chance?" he asked hopefully, though he very much doubted it.

"Sorry." She shook her head. The movement wrapped her lustrous short dark hair about her chin; her cocoa-brown eyes reflecting her regret. "I've heard a little about her from Gus, though I only moved here about a year ago."

"Gus?" His gaze narrowed on her as he probed for an answer. If Gus was a significant other, that might jinx his plans.

"Gus is good friend of mine." Rhia's eyes remained downcast as she reached for a second sandwich.

He wasn't cheered. It wasn't nearly enough information about this Gus person.

"Great sandwiches, by the way," he mumbled as he started on the plate of biscuits after her heartening nod, knowing he'd have to do better to get her to open up a bit more about her life here in the environs of Greywood Hall.

"So what does Gus know about Amelia Greywood?"

An answer followed after a miniscule hesitation. "Only that it's been years since the old lady lived at Greywood Hall, and that she was housebound for years before that."

Her reddened cheeks made Luke wonder what there was about this Gus that had her flushing. Was it because Gus was more than a good friend? That would really put a spanner in his works. He paced about before continuing, again appreciating the bright décor, the vases of wild flowers dotted around and the pictures on the walls. The scatter-rug beneath him was comfortably old, well flattened with years of treading feet.

"My lawyer tells me it's been around twelve years since Amelia went into Beechlee Nursing Home, and that the property has been unoccupied since then."

"That fits with what I've heard." She tracked his relentless movements. "Although I don't know any more about her."

He wondered how he could naturally bring the conversation around to find out just how much this Gus guy meant to her. He needed to know that fast. Turning back, he found her sitting patiently waiting for him to continue, her expressive face unable to mask her interest…in him.

That made him smile.

And she had been sort-of ogling him in the police car. Gus was in for a bad ride if this little sprite eyed-up every male she came in contact with. Luke decided Gus would be a total irrelevance, though a niggling irritation remained.

"As you've observed during your foray today…" His censure was intentional as he trod the rug in front of her, maintaining a penetrating eye contact. "Those dozen years haven't been kind to the property. It's a disgusting wreck."

His empty mug plonked down on her small coffee table, forcing her to follow his movements. The repugnance that mushroomed across his face was a disgust he couldn't mask. He could see it shocked her. His hands clenched over the back of the rocking chair he'd recently vacated as he glowered at the fireplace.

"The condition of the property bothers you?"

Her question seemed cautious, possibly to minimise offending him. Luke detected that, because she was not without manners, and when all was said and done, he was a complete stranger who was telling her some weirdly personal information.

"Of course it bloody does. It would disgust anyone with a grain of sense." He picked up the cushion from her rocking chair and punched it into submission, to aerate it, before he flopped down on the seat and deliberately placed it across his lap. The rocking of his chair played a rhythmic background as he mulled over the fireplace arrangement.

"Some people wouldn't look at it that way."

"What?" His feet firmed on the floor, halting the rock.

"Well…" Her reply was again guarded, forcing back his focus. "Some people would just value it for what it is."

"What that property is, is a bloody shame! You've seen the place. It's decaying by the minute."

"Yes, it is," she whispered. "But it's a charming old place, Luke. I've grown to love it."

"You love it? Now isn't that interesting." He relaxed back into a steady rock, his mood improving. "You made that conclusion based on your wandering today?" She'd unwittingly given him more fodder for his scheme to snare her services.

"Well, not exactly." Her reply was hesitant. Luke suspected she was being vigilant in not incriminating herself further.

Chapter Four

"Not exactly what? Not today?" Luke asked. "But on another day?" The tone was ruthless as he tossed the cushion aside, his gaze now firmly fixed on her.

"Yes. I have been there before, I admit it," Rhia answered.

Again, there was that profuse blush he was coming to admire a little too well.

"The place grows on you. I know it's dilapidated, though it must have been lovely once."

"Yes, Rhia. You mean a long time ago. And not just twelve years. That pile has been decaying for decades. Left to rot."

Relapsing into another subdued mood, he stared at the grate decoration. She withheld any further comments. He didn't blame her.

"Do you know by three a.m. this morning I was itching to come and view this decrepit pile?" His laugh was vigorous, though not happy. "My sleep patterns are always out of kilter when I return from Australia so I was awake. I couldn't wait till the rest of the UK woke up. My curiosity got the better of me and that doesn't happen often, I can assure you."

Relating how he'd jumped into his car, rather than waking his pilot and ordering his helicopter, he stopped when Rhia's tiny indrawn breath drew his focus. A derisive, doubtful expression had returned. His circumstances didn't meet her agreement? Her faintly scornful glower, the tiny raising of an eyebrow, was beginning to get to him yet he ploughed on.

"Of course that meant I arrived in the Yorkshire Dales around seven a.m. I made an exceptionally early check in to the Ruisdale Grange."

The slight clearing of her throat made him note both of her eyebrows rising up to almost meet her hairline. It was a quality hotel, one of a small chain he frequented, though nothing for her to get into a snit about.

"I rested for a couple of hours and then made my way to Amelia Greywood's lawyer to discover he was on holiday for the next two weeks. Though the guy had left most of his pressing casework with a junior colleague, the keys to Greywood Hall couldn't be located."

His laugh mocked. "They couldn't find the damn keys, Rhia! For a place like Greywood Hall? That should have warned me something was amiss, yet I was determined to see what I'd bloody well been landed with."

Her disapproving frown lacked sympathy.

"So you came anyway, to look for yourself?"

Something still soured her expression though he couldn't quite read it.

"Yes, after kicking my heels for a couple of hours to give the office more time to find the keys." He felt her recoil at his sarcasm. "Two hours. Do you realise how little there is to do there?" He named a local county town nearby.

"It's not exactly a throbbing metropolis, Luke, but I quite like that little market town."

Her response was filled with sufficient outrage to make him chortle as she endorsed it. "I've found everything I could want there since I moved away from London, on purpose."

"Point taken, Rhia." She might believe what she was saying though he didn't have to agree with her. "Suffice to say, it didn't occur to me that I wouldn't be able to get the keys to inspect the place."

He scrubbed his fingers across his chin stubble, failure being a novelty to him.

"Why hadn't you phoned ahead?"

"Good question." Luke laughed at himself. "Perhaps the fact that I left London at three in the morning had something to do with that?"

Rhia's sudden gleeful grin slayed him because she was now finding his predicament funny. Strange woman. He ploughed on, even more determined to get her on board his ludicrous venture.

"Anyway, I'm not known to be idle. I came to Greywood Hall to take a look around. I thought that even if I couldn't get into the house, I'd be able to see the grounds." The rocking chair played a steady thump on the wooden floor.

"But the main gates were locked when I first passed with Thor."

"Very true, the main gates were. I tried them first, though I didn't have metal cutters in my car, or anything to force the padlock, or break the chain with. It was the police who cut them open when they came to arrest me, Miss Ashton."

He waited though she ignored his little jibe. She eventually responded after a long tense silence.

"So how did you get in?"

Luke wondered how Rhia regularly got in as he answered.

"I found a back entrance to the stable block on the far side of the property, also padlocked of course. I left my car on the verge and nipped over the wall. From there, as you know already, I entered the house via that pantry window. It had a faulty catch that I was able to manipulate."

He felt his smile tighten up. "And the rest is history – except not quite."

"I don't understand why you were checking all the windows if you'd already broken into one. Your movements were pretty sneaky."

Her questioning was measured and purposeful. Needed the fine details tuned, did she? Well, he guessed she deserved to know since he needed her to help him one hundred per cent.

"It's my job," he answered, perusing the photographs hanging in a montage on her wall.

"What? But you said you weren't…"

"A burglar? Of course, I'm not." Encouraged by her naive responses sardonic laughter spilled forth. "I'm a Chartered Surveyor. My current focus in the UK is renovation of old properties."

"So you were checking all the windows as a professional?" That rosy little blush stained her cheeks, though he contrarily wished it hadn't. "I'm sorry about that."

Brushing off her apology with a terse wave of his hand, Luke enjoyed telling her more of his farcical story, though she had a cute little way of squirming up her nose when she was working something out, which distracted him from the main purpose.

"What did you mean 'and that's history, but not quite'?"

"My being willed the Hall isn't as straightforward as it seems. That's where you can help me."

He had a gut feeling she was going to be perfect for his needs.

"Me?"

Her bewilderment was exhilarating. He soared up in front of her.

"We've established that I'm not a burglar, but you, Miss Rhia Ashton, are a multiple trespasser." He let his index finger gently mock in front of her nose. "You've been trespassing on that property for some time." His tongue clicked against his teeth. "Disregarding the law."

"Gus told me it would be fine to walk Thor there." Her voice faded to nothing.

Creasing his dark eyebrows in doubt, Luke determined that this Gus person – whoever he was – needed to be eliminated from her life.

"Neither you, nor Gus had permission to be there. So here's the thing. Unless you want to go back to the police station and be charged with quite a few offences, I think you might need to listen to the proposal I'm about to put to you."

"But they said nothing at the police station about my trespassing. They brought me home."

Deliberately placing his hands on the chair back, one on each side of her shoulders, he effectively trapped her, finding she was easy to be near. He had to keep his mind out of his pants, though, because he needed Rhia Ashton to satisfy other needs.

She inched back from him, her head lolling on the cushion.

"Didn't you wonder why they let you go without a mention of the fact that you'd been wandering at will all over that property for ages? Doing who knows what damage?"

His gaze not wavering a single blink, he leaned conspiratorially closer.

"Of course, I wondered!" she cried. "But I never ever damaged anything."

"Well now, it's like this. You have me to thank for the lack of charges," he mocked, finding her lips were way too close for comfort. "I chose to tell them that they didn't need to proceed with the trespassing charges…for the foreseeable future."

"The foreseeable future?"

He persisted, knowing he was unnerving her. "Not for ever you understand, just for the coming months."

"Are you blackmailing me?"

"Blackmail?" He pulled back, calling a halt to her siren song. "You and me both. This is where the old lady excels. She has the last laugh."

Startled bewilderment battled with piqued interest as she leaned forward.

After a circuit of the room, he halted in front of her, one hand raking back his thick hair. She needed to be told all the facts. Well, perhaps not about the stupidly tight deadline: he could leave that little snippet till after she complied.

"Okay. I told you it's a bloody Dickensian nightmare. Here's the real deal, Rhia. I only become the completely legal owner of the property after I fulfil some very quirky terms which you can help me with."

"Me?"

A rabbit snagged in a deadly snare couldn't look more horrified. He was okay with that. He held up his hand in front of her.

"One." He pointed one finger at her. "I must reside at Greywood Hall with my spouse, for the period of one calendar year to eventually become the proud owner of this magnificently dilapidated property."

Her face blanched. He was almost sucked in by her indrawn breath as he continued checking off his list.

"Two." Another finger joined his first. "I need to do extensive renovations to Greywood Hall to live in it."

Rhia mutely nodded back.

"Three." Three fingers pointed at her, his response even more cynical. "I need to shell out a mountain of my own capital to do this since the old lady left the princely sum of six thousand four hundred and twenty four pounds which will barely pay for a replacement door knocker."

Luke waited while she digested that bit of information. A flicker of resentment flashed over her eyes. She looked fit to burst for some reason, though Luke admired the fact that she reined her control in. She remained silent till he waggled his three fingers close to her nose.

"Can you afford the restorations?"

Such a snippy little cat.

"Of course, I damned well can! I've got more than plenty money to do that. Plenty even for the hugely exorbitant death taxes that will no doubt be involved."

"More than plenty?" Her expression sneered. "Some people would think six thousand four hundred and twenty four pounds was a fortune."

Luke couldn't credit how livid her face was. A reaction he hadn't expected, yet he quite liked it. Her criticism was on a roll. Highly entertaining, and not what he was used to.

"If you've got loads of money then what's your problem?" She bristled as she slipped forward to verbally attack him, her eyes molten ire. "You might well have to use your own money in the first instance, but you'll have an absolutely delightful property at the end of it which will be worth its weight in gold. Then you can fob it off and make your millions if you want. What the hell have you got to complain about?"

He found her passion impressive.

"I don't have a money problem." He moved in on her again. "The problem is that right this minute I don't have a wife. And if I don't have a wife, I can't fulfil these ridiculous terms."

"Oh, I see."

He could tell the exact moment when she willed herself to calm down and focus properly on the immediate matters at hand.

"But if you've no wife and it's going to cost you a lot of money anyway, why don't you just say 'no thank you' and walk away from the legacy if it bothers you this much?"

Luke trapped her focus once more as he stepped back into her sphere. "I knew you'd be smart and ask good questions." He leaned his whole body towards hers. "With your knowledge of history, his hand swept out towards the bookcase filled with historical texts, I'm absolutely sure you'll appreciate this little snippet."

Her hitched breath distracted him.

"As in all good Dickensian stories the old lady isn't finished yet. If I don't do anything at all with the property, after a period of fifty years, I'm told, it will revert to the crown."

"That won't matter to you, will it?" Rhia seemed fixated on his lips.

"Of course it will. How could I ignore such a valuable property?"

Disappointment flashed. Her cheeks tightened. "You've totally lost me. Do you want it, or not?"

"It would be a crying shame to leave that house to rot for another fifty years. It's a valuable house and valuable land, and it could be converted to multiple uses for corporate business, or as a hotel facility."

"Ah…future revenues?" That impressive derision had returned.

"Rhia, you wouldn't want to be responsible for that venerable old house to fall into even more disrepair: a house you've already professed to love? Would you want that on your conscience? Knowing it was your fault that it happened?"

"My fault?"

"Nobody can do anything at all to pull that property back to glory except me. I'm ready to take on the responsibility of restoring that so lovable heap of rubble, though I need your help to do it."

He could almost see her brain working through the implications.

"If you have to restore it as a domestic domicile, could you still use it afterwards? For business use, without needing to do loads of further renovations that would cost you more money?"

"Well, that's another quandary, isn't it?" Luke lapsed into silence.

Rhia hesitated before adding, "I appreciate what you are saying, though how does it all affect me?"

"I don't have a wife, and I sure as hell hadn't been planning on having one anytime soon."

"So, you can't inherit right now. But you could if you got married?"

"Bang on," he chuckled.

He gently grasped her fingers, encouraging her to her feet. "But not later. I never hang around and waste valuable time. It has to be as soon as possible, as early as can be arranged."

"What?"

"Why should we let the property deteriorate further?" He pulled back when he discovered his fingers absently caressing hers. "You know you can't back away and let that lovely old estate you profess to love fall into complete ruin."

"What are you talking about?"

"I need someone to marry me. Immediately. And I think that person should be you."

Rhia wilted down into the chair and leaned back against the cushions, her eyes clouded with confusion. "Why would you want me to marry you?"

Luke moved away to look out the window, needing to create a little distance.

"I've just told you I need a woman right away, to marry me and cohabit with me at Greywood Hall for a year, so that I can do something with that dilapidated pile. Someone who knows this deal from the outset. And you're convenient."

***

"I'm convenient?"

Rhia could barely answer; she was so offended by his glib remark. What an asshole he was to say something like that.

He turned back to her. "You're not already married, are you?"

"No. I'm not married."

Her teeth were almost glued together, resentment thick. What did the smooth slimy slug mean by convenient?

"You live next door and it just so happens you're also my tenant," Luke informed her.

The greasy toad didn't even acknowledge her horrified gasp.

"That should work out very handy for the first week or so."

Only good manners prevented her from telling him to damned well go to hell, or at the very least sit still for a moment so that she could listen properly as he briskly meandered around the furniture. She tried to follow his train of thought, not sure of anything except being annoyed that his crazy plans were twistedly intriguing.

"I need a wife immediately so that I can ensure that the property doesn't fall to bits, and I know you don't want that to happen since you profess to already love the mouldering ruin."

She wasn't thrilled at the prospect of the house in total decay, though what made him think she'd just fall in with his implausible plans.

"And you know what, Rhia?"

Luke had changed tack. Had she missed something important?

"Your profession is also convenient."

"My profession?"

She was flabbergasted. First she was convenient because she lived next door and now because of her job? What the hell did the pesky man think she did for a living?

He then astounded her by his detailed knowledge of her work history.

"You have the perfect historical research skills for finding out the history of Greywood Hall, and for sleuthing out why the hell I'm the one who's been chosen to inherit the dilapidated pile. Because that's something I don't damned well know, and sure as shit definitely want to!"

She couldn't suppress the interest from flickering at his mention of researching such an esteemed old place as Greywood Hall. To be given free rein there would be an absolute heaven.

"And let me tell you now," he ranted, "I don't for one minute think that unravelling why it's me will be an easy task for anyone. That house up there is like a bloody junk yard. Every room is totally cluttered with hundreds of years of trivia, and god knows what."

His voice rose with exasperation and, she thought, almost unwilling…passion. He was searching for the best words to describe the place.

"…and you know what else?"

It was meant as a rhetorical question because he lumbered on, not giving her a shred of a chance to respond.

"I damned well can't get rid of a single piece of paper in case it happens to be the very one that says why I'm the beneficiary."

Luke's disgust was almost palpable, yet contrarily Rhia's curiosity was now well-fired. "Junk yard?" Every room full of historical artefacts just waiting to be exposed? Oh, my! The palpitations.

Maybe his proposal wasn't so off after all?

While she was pondering her principles he continued, still padding around.

"You can think of our marriage like one of your contracts. You'll just be living at Greywood Hall as my wife while you're doing all the research."

"As your wife? And also your researcher?" Rhia couldn't formulate any other questions. As a historian the research was so very, very tempting.

Luke halted his pacing and grinned at her, his convinced expression revealing his realisation that the carrot he'd just dangled was something she wanted to nibble. He was enthused by the concept, but she wasn't too sure about it, or about him. Not yet. What she did know was that he wasn't finished as his words tripped out like fine oil.

"Living up at Greywood Hall while you research the place will be a marvellous experience for you. Just think about it. All those knickknack filled rooms." His chuckle became a full bodied roll. "And I'm not kidding about them, Rhia. Every single room. Loads of them."

She willed her features to remain impassive though it was hard to suppress the growing excitement. Being the first person to research all the prime sources at Greywood?

Unbelievable!

"The estate is a living history book," Luke explained, animated about it, though she was well aware that some of his enthusiasm was fabricated to sway her. "I mean literally." His sudden grin was compelling, "The whole place is amazing. On the nursery floor I found original copies of children's classics, leather-bound versions like The Lost World by Conan Doyle." His eyes flashed fire. "That's exactly what the house is like." He stopped right in front of her and clutched her shoulders, almost crushing her in his intensity. "It's a lost world that needs rediscovering by an expert. You're the expert it needs so badly."

His fingers absently gentled, his gaze willing her to imagine it all with him. "The only one who can help find that lost world again is you. You'll only have to be in it for five seconds to absorb its ancient pages and you'll want to read to the very end."

The bizarre picture he painted tempted her and set her heart racing.

"It's an astonishing place. You can't possibly miss such a fabulous opportunity."

His next deadpan, staccato phrases were another shocker.

"Of course the opposite of being my wife and researcher, and living up at the Hall with me as your husband, is that you might have to leave this cottage. I might want it for another tenant – like myself initially, or for one of my workers."

Rhia gagged again at his audacity. He was the most mercurial man she'd ever met. She equally loathed him and admired his cunning at the same time. The man was deranged yet she was entertaining his ideas? What a bleeding idiot she was.

Well…maybe not quite so duped.

"You'd evict me?" Surely not? Unfortunately, his moods had already been so unpredictable that day; she hadn't a clue what she could expect from him.

"As your landlord I could do that." Luke nodded his head emphatically. "Then again there's the little matter of prosecution."

"You, bastard! That's definitely blackmail."

"Only sort of." He was thoroughly enjoying her outrage. "On the other hand you'd get huge benefits if we married." He smiled a small calculating smile.

"You're stark raving bonkers! You can't want to marry me." She sank back into the cushions of the chair.

"I do," he answered smoothly, as though it was the simplest thing in the world to say.

"You don't even know me. You don't love me."

"Come on, Rhia. Who said anything about love?" His cynical tone wasn't lost on her. "I don't need to love you to have a bit of paper that says I'm married to you." Moving over to the window he casually looked out to her small front garden.

Whirling back to her, plans urgently dripped off his tongue. "Think about it like this. We get married. You stay free of prosecution, and you can walk Thor all over the place every single day. I'll guarantee you employment as my researcher for a whole year. I'll even give you double the salary you presently earn, and later on you can move back here to this cottage. A whole year's worth of double earnings, doesn't that sound good, Rhia?"

A year's worth of employment was persuasive. She was just building her Find Your Family research business, and since coming to the Yorkshire Dales, contracts had been hard to come by.

Luke was pacing again. He really was quite the schemer. She was impressed, in spite of the fact that he was a total dreamer.

"I can rearrange my current schedules to suit. We can stay here in your well-located cottage for the first few days, as I renovate the property. That way I can be on hand, as it were."

She watched him rub his hands together as he strode his now well-worn circuit around her mismatched furniture.

"As soon as a few rooms are habitable in Greywood Hall we can move in, live there for one year while the rest is being restored, and then when the property is mine to do with as I choose, you can move back to your life here in the cottage." His pragmatic tone matched his candid words.

"You're crazy! That's coercion." Her hackles rose, because this man really did mean business. "Why would I marry you? I don't even know you."

"Rhia, you don't need to know me. You don't need to love me. You just have to sign the paper that says you're my wife." Luke continued to catalogue the details as he stood in front of her.

She was outraged at his callous plans, yet needed time to think. A lot of what he said was lucrative for potential earnings and for valuable experience.

"I'd have to put my personal life on hold for a whole year." She wasn't going to tell him that her personal life probably wouldn't be much different from the last year, and that by choice she'd had zilch social life since moving to the isolated cottage.

"It's only a year."

She deliberately shut her eyes on his sassy twinkle so that she could regroup; think her way through this bizarre proposal or whatever the hell it was. She felt his breath on her cheeks when he bent forward to whisper.

"It's not that long."

Her stomach clenched. Live with this man then say a casual goodbye after a year? If she started to live with this man, she didn't think an eternity would be enough. If it was only a paper marriage that might be worse! Her eyes jerked open. "You can't expect me to do that."

"Sure I can," Luke replied looking oddly pleased by her denial. "Of course if you're not willing to follow those plans then I'll easily find another woman." His head cocked to the side, contemplating the idea. "To marry me, I mean."

The man was yanking her chain. He'd never be short of arm candy.

He continued to rile her. "I know lots of women who would be happy to help me fulfil the terms of the will as my wife, though absolutely none of them will be any good at all with helping me unravel the history of the place. None of them could assist with the restoration or find out why I'm the beneficiary."

She was highly aware of him as his eyes flicked over her tight cycling shorts and cheap T-shirt but was then gob smacked when hurtful mirth curled his lip.

"My girlfriends tend to be very decorative – none of them could be considered bluestocking material."

Fury gripped her. How dared he compare her to the airheads he probably always consorted with? She wasn't anything much to look at with her short legs and not much bust to speak of, but how could he be so dismissive and cruel?

Luke strolled away. She glared at his retreating back pretty sure many of the women he'd known would leap at the chance to be married to him for a year, yet she wasn't so naïve. His bubbly flirts would contrive to milk him for all they could get after that year was up. Well. Hell mend him! He deserved one of his 'don't I look beautiful' empty vessels to rip him off. She had to get rid of the bloody man before she totally combusted. Greywood Hall would just have to moulder away, for there was no way she would marry such an arrogant pig.

Greywood Hall?

How could she do that to the poor neglected house?

She had to think. She wasn't an airhead…she had a brain somewhere among the mess of emotions she was right at that moment. She closed her eyes to regroup yet again.

"Rhia." Luke's soft inquiry made her eyes flick open again. "It's a good offer."

Why was she unable to resist the temptation?

"Of course, if I marry some other woman, I suppose you could still do the research for me, and live up at Greywood Hall with myself and my new wife."

As if she'd consider that.

"Though I guess that might depend on what would happen after the marriage. Maybe three of us living there would become too…” He padded around, again leaving the end of his sentence hanging.

Rhia pushed any thoughts of prosecution, coercion and blackmail onto the back burner. She cleared her throat encouraging him to cease his pacing and turn back to face her. She levelled his stare, very guarded with her words.

“So, are you saying that since you don’t need love for this marriage, it would be a business arrangement? Till you’re the legal owner? Then we’d separate? It wouldn’t be a real marriage?” She wanted Luke to see she’d have no flannelling or prevarication.

“Your words, not mine. I wouldn’t call what we’d do together just business…it would be more of an accommodation of needs.”

“An accommodation?” She wondered what the hell that meant. “We’d cohabit at Greywood Hall as man and wife, without love, for a year, and lead separate lives?”

“Not exactly.” A small smile tweaked the side of his mouth, betraying his amusement. “I think the answer to that is dependent on your interpretation of love. I don’t expect love, but I do expect sex during the coming year.”

Rhia’s face flamed at his candid assessment.

He nodded. “It could be more of a mutual agreement where you and I share our daily lives, sex happening for me whenever it happens, till after the year is up, then we’d stop the arrangement.”

“For a year?” She remained rooted in place, though her whole body frizzled.

“That’s what it will take to fulfil the requirements of the will. Then the property will eventually be mine.”

He moved closer and leaned in. Barely a hairbreadth separated them now.

Chapter Five

"You would seem to be getting a lot more out of this arrangement than I would." Rhia's chin hitched up as she faced him.

Luke stepped back from her and whirled away. His voice grew softer, evaluating, as he walked towards the window.

"Well, let's see. Apart from no criminal record, and no resultant slur on your character, when I sell the place I'd be prepared to make you a financial settlement when we get divorced, as well as turning over the title deeds to the cottage. You'd become the owner."

"What if I don't want your money?" Rhia was appalled at his attitude yet stuck to her ground.

"Then we'd say goodbye amicably." He launched back into pacing once more.

Rhia's brain whirred, trying to regain some equilibrium, though her heart was hammering. "So let me clarify this again. We'd live together at Greywood Hall for a year. As man and wife. Then I'd say goodbye to the arrangement."

He stopped. "Yes."

"During that year you expect to have intimate relations?"

She eyeballed him as close as one can do with a foot in height difference between them, seeing a heated spark darkening the lush green of his irises.

"You mean sex with someone, Rhia? Naturally, I'd expect over a year to have lots of sex."

"So, lots of sex."

Rhia sweated, aiming for the same business like tone. "And would you stay here at Greywood Hall all the time?"

Luke stopped, facing away from her probing eyes, his voice becoming muffled. "I don't think so – it's too far away from my main offices for that to be practical, and I travel a lot." He paused to glance out of the window as a heavy vehicle passed along the lane, one of the very few that had passed since Luke entered the cottage. "Though, I believe, the will stipulates that Greywood Hall has to be my main domicile, so I imagine I'd need to be here quite a lot of the time."

He'd also be away from home…quite a lot. Making love to other women. The mere thought horrified Rhia. She couldn't, and wouldn't, ever share a man with anyone else again, whether it was a business arrangement or a real one. That dart had already sailed. She could only be in a relationship with a man who was one hundred per cent hers, and hers alone. What had happened in the past must never ever occur again. She looked at her feet as she mouthed her next words.

"So are you saying that you'd expect me to be your researcher by day and your dutiful wife waiting for you at your stately home at night? Your woman in residence?"

He cleared his throat, his answer a soft sigh.

"That about sums it up."

"When you're on your travels? What then?" she challenged.

"What do you mean? What then?" He crept towards her, but she shrank away, needing his answer.

"When you're away from home, to London or Australia, or wherever, would you expect to have sex with other women there because we just have…an accommodation?" Her eye contact was unflinching, even though it cost her enormous effort to do so. It amazed her that she managed to keep her tone neutral, especially when her insides were rebelling.

Luke barely blinked, though she could tell he was wondering where her conversation was leading.

"I have in the past had sex in Australia, and other places."

"So, if you're away from home and having sex in those other places, then I would have the same possibility for affairs here?" Her words were deliberate, her focus determined, because she wasn't giving way on this.

"While you're away that is?"

Luke's face was almost totally wiped of expression. Eventually he turned his back on her and looked at her bookshelves. "Are you talking about Gus? Or somebody else as well?"

"Maybe." Rhia felt her face glowing. The mere thought of having sex with Gus was ludicrous, yet she was nettled by Luke's pat attitude.

"I've not lived like a monk, but I don't have multiple relationships going on at the same time."

"Would you please clarify that for me?"

He turned back to her, his gaze penetrating, his words dragged through gritted teeth.

"I'm saying that I only have a sexual relationship with one woman at a time. Regardless of which continent I'm on."

"So if you were married to me for a year, and for some reason we had sex, would you be prepared for me to be the only woman you'd have sex with during that time?" Rhia knew she must sound mad, like a dog worrying a very juicy bone.

"What exactly are you asking?" An unexplained vitality lit his eyes.

Rhia couldn't stand still any longer. She too paced though nowhere near Luke, unable to look him in the eye when she uttered her next tentative words.

"I would just be a convenience – your little wife at home – with the possibility of sex on tap."

She was now the one padding around the room, her nerves pinging and fit to snap. "I want something which will clarify this temporary relationship of ours. Under the circumstances you're coercing me into I will marry you, though only if I have it in writing that I'll be your only lover during the time we are married."

"You're asking for some kind of prenuptial agreement?"

"Prenuptial agreement? Don't be ridiculous," Rhia scoffed.

"That isn't what you mean?" She watched Luke's mouth twitching.

"Not if that's some sort of way of extorting money from you." She flushed with embarrassment that he should think that of her. That she'd be so mercenary. "I don't want any of your money, Luke, but if you expect me to enter into this farce, then I do want some assurance that you won't be bringing diseases home to me."

Although the words left her mouth easily she knew she did, in her own way, have some money-driven reasons for agreeing.

To be employed for a whole year was a very nice carrot, even at her normal rate never mind twice her earnings. The cottage belonging to her was too good to pass up on because she still had to clear up debts incurred by the lazy good-for-nothing boyfriend who had milked her of her savings.

To research the house and the Greywood family and possibly even have some input in the restorations was a fabulous prospect and could lead to a lot of future business.

To get her teeth into solving the mystery of Amelia Greywood's choice of Luke as the inheritor was actually much more appealing than any amount of money, since during her walks around the grounds she had wondered plenty of times about its history.

"And if I don't meet this requirement of yours?" Luke probed.

Storming right up to him, stopping a hairbreadth away, her answer was unequivocal. "If you're not prepared to meet that request then you can darned well take me to the police right now because no marriage will take place." The words rapped out, over her arms held up crossed at the wrists.

He seemed amused, yet remained silent.

Dropping her tense fingers to cradle her hips, she continued, "Or, if you say you'll be monogamous and you fail to keep to the requirement during the year, I'll start divorce proceedings and we will go our own ways. And if I go, you won't meet the conditions of the will."

"If I don't have Greywood Hall, it won't be restored properly." Luke's palms cupped her shoulders. "You don't want that to happen."

Shrugging out of his grasp Rhia stepped back, hoping the passion in her response couldn't be heard. "No. You won't have Greywood Hall and you won't have me either."

Deliberately turning her back on him, she didn't understand why that thought upset her. She'd barely met the man, yet he was having an incredibly profound effect on her.

"Now who's blackmailing whom?"

Luke's words whispered from directly behind her, his huge body moving closer to cradle her without making contact. Then she sensed him reaching for her. Resting his hands on her shoulders his thumbs gently kneaded the tension at the back of her neck before turning her round. She couldn't prevent the shivers.

"Rhia."

"I want…"

"I know what you want." Luke's head tilted forward.

An insistent buzz interrupted.

"The telephone…" She struggled out of his arms.

"Ignore it!" He tried to draw her back.

"No. I'm sorry. I should never have said…" She was barely coherent as she tore out of the room to pick up the phone.

***

Luke heard her respond to the caller as he watched her out in the hallway.

"Gus! Hello."

Her cheery tone chilled him like an arctic breeze. He watched her turn towards him, the landline trembling in her hand. Her smile of welcome for Gus gutted him: she was so pleased to take the call. A knife twisted somewhere.

"No, I'm fine. It was all a dreadful mistake."

What was a mistake? The woman was proving to be an unexpected and delightful challenge. He wanted to start their partnership right that very minute.

"No, no Gus. Honestly."

Rhia's laugh echoed out in the corridor.

"I really don't need anything."

Luke scowled. She couldn't really be this genuine. She must want something, women always did. He'd wanted to see how grasping she'd be over his proposals, but she'd thrown him a loop by issuing her own demands. A spitting little hind she'd been, bluntly demanding he not be a rutting stag.

He was tickled by the thought that her words might be prompted by jealousy over him having sexual relations with another woman. She was so soft, so fragile, yet in many ways so feistily strong.

Though she'd blown him off – for Gus. Luke's teeth grated.

Her laugh echoed again, the husky sound now irritating. "No charges. No repercussions."

This Gus person had somehow heard that she'd ended up at the police station. As Rhia nattered on he wanted to punch something, preferably Gus, but as to consequences? The little pixie didn't know the half of it yet. However, she would.

"Yes, okay. I'll catch up with you later," she chuckled. "Love you, too."

She carefully put the handset down before coming back in to the sitting room, her embarrassment obvious.

"Luke. I'm really sorry." She was unable to look him squarely in the eye now. "I don't know what I was thinking."

Stepping right in front of her, he slipped his palms up to cup her shoulders. "We have a deal, Rhia."

"We have a deal?"

She looked so confused. She'd rejected his advances so it wasn't surprising she was baffled. He forced her to look at him.

"We'll get married as soon as I can arrange it. We'll take up residence at Greywood Hall as soon as is feasible. We'll live as man and wife in the full sense of the words. If I have a lover it will only be you, and I'll be your only lover. You'll have the satisfaction of seeing the property fully restored, and be able to roam freely with your dog, every single day, knowing you aren't trespassing."

Her face turned pale at the word trespassing.

"But you can forget Gus and anybody else during that time." He wanted no misinterpretation. "I'll let you know about the arrangements as soon as possible."

He took himself off before she could respond.

***

An official contract duly arrived the next day before ten a.m., hand delivered by Luke's PA. Rhia found Jeremy to be a likeable guy who, from first introduction, demonstrated he knew all the particulars of the extremely outlandish deal.

He conducted their meeting with considerable aplomb. His curious gaze appraised her, though he never strayed from the professional, not making inquiries that were too personal as he worked their way through the simple but legal terms on the contract. Yet he did ask some mildly confusing questions, questions which made Rhia wonder about their relevance.

"How long have you lived at Border Cottage?" Jeremy asked.

"Around a year ago I relocated here. July the second."

"Have you made any recent trips in the last two weeks?" He scribbled on the pad lying on his knees.

"No," Rhia was bemused. "So long as you don't count my occasional trips to the supermarket in Skipton."

He chuckled. "No, I think we'll discount those trips. I was meaning some holiday perhaps?"

She'd had no holidays at all since she moved to the cottage. A few more questions about recent days and her current work schedules were simple to answer, her mind drifting to wonder how the heck Luke had organised the contract since he must have had his London lawyers work on it the minute he'd left her the previous afternoon.

Rhia began to realise what Luke had indicated seemed true – he didn't like to watch the grass grow. Not only was she aware of the power of the man, she was becoming more aware of what he could achieve with the power of money.

Unable to find fault with it, she duly signed the contract. It had been pre-signed by Luke who had indeed included an incontestable monogamy clause, and after penning her signature the paperwork was countersigned by Jeremy.

She was loathe to hand over her birth certificate when requested. It was necessary to prove her identity for the marriage licence, yet her fingers lingered on it, her whole hand shaking so much Jeremy had to ease it out of her grasp. At that point the bizarre undertaking became so real. She was signing away her identity. For a year!

Jeremy's tone was designed to soothe her frantic heartbeat, though her appreciation was vague at best. "Luke's a good employer, Miss Ashton. He's tough but fair, and however weird this deal might seem, you can trust him. If he puts something on paper, he'll stick to the letter. Now, can I make sure I have your home and mobile numbers?"

"The signals are absolute pants around here. I regularly lose contact. The landline is much more reliable."

"We'll work around that, don't worry." Jeremy sounded so sure.

"Luke has some fancy satellite, never fail communications?"

"Something akin to that." Jeremy's smile was genuine, though the man was discreet.

All was done and dusted by ten fifteen.

The rest of the day passed where she wanted to see Luke but also dreaded it too, unable to believe she'd agreed to marry a man she'd only known for a couple of hours.

Barely functioning, she continually chewed over what had already happened, what hadn't quite happened, and what might happen. She took out her bank statement and stared at the state of her finances. That made her feel only marginally better about what she'd done.

It wasn't a quiet day though, not with the unusual sounds of a helicopter nearby, and the steady flow of vehicles that passed her door.

Out of sheer contrariness she walked Thor in the opposite direction from Greywood Hall twice that day, maintaining firm control over his movements. She needed to keep him close to heel to be safe with the increased traffic. After both sojourns, she was frustrated. She wasn't at all sure what she'd been trying to prove by going that way, because she was definitely curious about what was happening in the other direction.

Of Luke, she heard not a cheep. She'd expected him to at least call and talk to her, but that didn't happen. She went to bed feeling very out of sorts.

The landline phone rang early the following morning, at just after seven. Rhia was awake and nursing her second cup of coffee. Her sleep had been fitful and then the rumble of heavy trucks that passed her door, starting just after six, ruined any further chance of dozing. For a quiet little backwater neighbourhood, the vehicular activity could only be put down to one reason. Luke. The traffic must all be going to Greywood Hall.

She was grumpy when she lifted the receiver.

"Meet me here at the Ruisdale Grange for lunch, Rhia." Luke's brusque tone made it sound like an order rather than an invitation.

Frustrated with the speed at which events were taking place, and annoyed at being ignored the day before, she listened without comment, only answering when he informed her that a driver would be along to pick her up.

"No." Her tone was resolute. "I'll drive myself, thank you." She knew how to get to the top class hotel though she'd never had the opportunity, or quite frankly the cash, to sample its exclusive grandeur.

On arrival, her breath hitched. Luke stood sentinel at the top of the short flight of stairs by the entryway. He was every bit as hunky as she'd thought two days before. The expensive dark suit he wore was faultless, a collar and tie neatly in place – very formal. He stood as though he was master of all he surveyed as he talked on his phone.

This man was way out of her league.

Her composure deflated: she felt nervous and exposed…and very trapped. She'd had plenty of time that morning to consider what she'd said she'd do. Unfortunately, she wasn't convinced she could now follow through on her agreement. The research part of the contract she'd have absolutely no issue with at all. Living in the same house, she could probably manage. Though being contract lovers and then say goodbye? Like sex buddies where partners only arranged to meet for recreational or stress-busting sex? For a whole year? That was the bit she wasn't now sure of, even though being monogamous lovers had been her suggestion. She was attracted to him and that meant casual was impossible. She liked to know she was in control of what she was doing, but this situation was now way out of her control.

Luke had seen her approach and had pocketed his mobile. She couldn't back out now and slip off home, so swallowing her insecurity she straightened her spine and drew nearer, stemming the trembles that threatened to make her trip over the cobbles of the driveway. She always fulfilled obligations. Somehow she'd do it.

***

Rhia was lovely. Perversely Luke didn't want her to be so attractive.

Personally, all he needed was her name on the dotted line on their marriage certificate. Professionally, he needed her considerable research skills because he now knew she'd had a glowing career as a research assistant with great future possibilities at the Victoria and Albert Museum in London, where she'd gone after graduation from Oxford. Only the very best got such plum jobs, but something had made her resign from those great prospects to come to live in the Yorkshire Dales and set up her own internet business.

Plenty of people did that kind of thing, of course, they did, though what could her motivations be for moving from the metropolitan area to the boondocks? He didn't yet know, but in the fullness of time he'd find out.

Pragmatically speaking, if he needed to be married to someone for a year it would be better all round if he could get on with the woman on a daily basis. Though, to actually physically desire the person? That was something else entirely.

On leaving the police station two days previously, he'd geared himself up to go through with a paper marriage only. He'd planned to compensate her highly, but to his surprise she only seemed fixed on her monogamy clause. His track record at being with a woman for longer than a couple of months wasn't great. Something always soured his relationships almost as soon as they began.

This time though a whole calendar year was at stake. Whatever it was that made him restless with previous lovers he'd have to suppress, manage it somehow, or sharing the same space for twelve months would become a huge problem.

Rhia walked towards him wearing a slinky suit of rich bronze and sexily high ankle-strapped shoes that emphasised her slim legs. The fitted skirt swept just above her knees leaving plenty of leg to savour and the tight nipped-in jacket accentuated her curves. The day before he'd wanted to call her, but he'd quelled those urges because he needed her long-term cooperation. Instead he'd turned to planning and plotting.

She wasn't smiling as she walked to him. She looked angry, like she'd sounded when on the phone earlier that morning. One thing was certain; she wasn't pleased to see him. He had been gearing up to enjoy a kiss of welcome. Now that wasn't going to work. Wiping the smile from his face he forced himself to hold back.

"Hello, Rhia."

With a tight parody of a smile he led her through the hotel foyer, escorting her to a table which already awaited them in the main restaurant, barely giving her time to draw breath. A hovering waiter immediately performed services with napkins and menus, another waiter coming for their initial drinks order.

"Sparkling water, please," Luke ordered, not waiting for a response from her before launching into his plans for the next few days. The bristling porcupine of that first day had definitely returned. "I went to see the local Superintendent Registrar early on today, to make arrangements for a special licence, so that our marriage ceremony can be here at the Ruisdale Grange first thing tomorrow morning." He kept the tone level and businesslike.

Her little gasp of dismay wasn't as quiet as he thought she intended. Luke feared things might not go as smooth as he'd hoped.

"How can it possibly be tomorrow? You need three weeks for wedding banns to be read."

She appeared dazed at the speed he was taking over her life. He guessed that nerves must be getting the better of her. "Not so, Rhia."

Her face was thunderous, though it got even worse when he explained. "You've been resident in this district for more than the required seven days. It only takes one of us to have done that, and it only took one of us to proffer the necessary certification and make the request for us to get married with a special licence for tomorrow. As of this morning, I gave the required one day's notice."

"What?"

She couldn't seem to absorb his words.

"This hotel is registered for the performance of wedding ceremonies and I've persuaded the Registrar to marry us at seven forty-five tomorrow morning, giving her time to get back to the Registry for her next scheduled marriage ceremony at nine."

"What?"

Diners around them turned interested ears at her pitch, though Rhia was oblivious to them.

"Normal people don't get married after one day," she railed, her tone pretty bloody-minded about it all.

"I don't consider I need to do what normal people do, Rhia."

He tracked her agitation as she huffed, and looked everywhere but at him. "You've got that right. You're not normal!"

Unfortunately, he hadn't factored in the possibility she'd reject any of his preparations. What was getting her in such a fit of temper? She'd happily signed on the dotted line the day before, according to Jeremy, whom Luke had sourly noted had been quite enthusiastic about Rhia's attraction.

A tense silence reigned till Rhia blurted, "What if I wanted to get married in a church?" Her agitated fingers twirled a fork around, tapping it against the table as she awaited his response.

"I suppose a church ceremony could be arranged, somehow, if it's what you want," Luke answered, wanting to soothe her. She was complex, different from any woman he'd before had dealings with. Perhaps a little hasty, he'd already set the wheels rolling for claiming his inheritance, so there was no way she could be allowed to back out. He forced his tone to level and softened his expression, made it appear more amenable. "I've looked into this thoroughly and have taken the quickest route possible."

"Oh, I suppose anywhere will do." Her fingers had started on the napkin. If had it been paper, and not super quality linen, it would be shredded. "Though not tomorrow."

She was adamant, not at all the flexible woman he thought she'd be.

"I need some more notice than that."

She was back to huffing. He heard even more panic in her voice now.

"You can't expect me to agree to tomorrow."

She was so stressed Luke decided maybe he'd been a little precipitate in arranging for a registrar to marry them the next day. He hadn't expected such vehement resistance. The clause in the will stating his claim on the estate had to happen within thirty-one days, he'd doggedly kept to himself. There was no need for Rhia to know that information, even if it did seem a bit duplicitous not to tell her. His usual fair-minded conscience only pricked a little.

"I need a little more time."

Luke's nod was reluctant. "Saturday then. We'll get married this Saturday." Already his mind had worked out the cancellations and rescheduling he'd need to do. Not to mention persuading the Registrar yet again.

There was a definite gulp from Rhia. He couldn't help but hear it.

"No. We'll compromise," she insisted, clearly unwilling to back down. "Make it twelve days from now. That's half of the time that normal people wait."

"Not quite. Make it eleven days." Luke was amazed. She was dead serious. He was reluctantly impressed by her bargaining. Her jaw was set antagonistically, though in a strange way her tenacity added to her allure. She was the most unpredictable female he'd ever encountered. He acquiesced. Since the lawyer had granted the usual three weeks declaration of banns her time scale still fit in easily with that requirement. "Okay. We'll have the ceremony in twelve days."

Good manners prevailed as she nodded. "Thank you. You said you were sorting out other things this morning?"

"I'm taking you for a dress fitting at three-thirty this afternoon to a highly recommended wedding shop in Derby. We'll leave after lunch, and you can choose your dress and other necessities."

"No."

"What do you mean, no?"

Luke was puzzled. Didn't women always want to go shopping for dresses on unlimited budgets? In the past he'd occasionally paid for previous girlfriends to go and buy something suitable for a special function. He didn't quite have a word for how he felt about Rhia's rebuff. He acknowledged the circumstances of the wedding were very unorthodox, though it still seemed to him to require some sort of effort. He'd geared himself up to accompany Rhia to select a dress. He was well aware that it wasn't exactly the traditional thing for the groom to accompany the bride to choose those garments, but it seemed the thing to do given the occasion.

"No."

Rhia's tone brooked no argument. In fact she sounded so much like the peremptory matron at his boarding school he almost gagged, because that woman had been a real harridan.

"I'll organise my own dress, thank you," she persisted, "and you'll not pay for it, or any other accoutrement I buy for our so called wedding. I'm not a paid whore, though I'm beginning to wonder about that now. I'll enter into this marriage because I said I would, for the refurbishment of Greywood Hall, though I'll do it in my own way." Her chin was firm. "And anyway it would take forever to get to Derby."

"Not by helicopter. My helicopter can pick us up in about an hour."

"Helicopter? Now why didn't I think of that?"

Luke was exasperated with her sarcasm. He realised he'd need to compromise a little more to get his own way. Things weren't going according to plan. He didn't normally do concessions, yet he'd made one already in her monogamy clause. Irritation made him terse.

"I'll cancel the appointment then, if you'll excuse me just a moment?"

Chapter Six

The merest nod was her assent.

Luke gave Jeremy brief instructions to cancel the afternoon plans and the registrar for the following morning. Then Rhia heard him tell Jeremy the wedding was still on, just not the following day, but to reschedule the registrar for twelve days hence.

That was it?

A few words were all it took to cancel a wedding, a helicopter and a specialist dress fitting.

After re-pocketing his phone he continued outlining plans. "I've asked Jeremy to be a witness to our marriage. Is there someone you'd like to ask to be the second witness?"

"No. Of course not. This isn't a real marriage so I'm not asking any of my friends to attend such an absurd situation," Rhia answered, her tone flat. "And I've no immediate relatives that I need bother about."

Her fingers smoothed the pristine white tablecloth, needing something to do to quell her still frayed nerves. She could face up to the consequences of her trespassing, or she could sign her life away for a year.

"Would you prefer me to arrange the second witness too?" Luke was sounding annoyed.

"Yes. I would like you to arrange another witness, although I don't imagine you'll want to be asking your parents, or other relatives, to this charade either."

"My parents are both dead, so I won't be inviting them." Cynicism loaded his tone. "Roger – he's my London butler – will be happy to do the job."

"Your butler?" Rhia couldn't prevent her tongue from rattling on. "Of course. I'm perfectly sure your London butler would be delighted to perform such service for you."

He probably had another in Australia. Inwardly, she reeled at the opulence of his life. Butler. Helicopter. Ferrari. This rich man lived an existence nothing like hers. She couldn't possibly measure up to his standards. What was she doing entering into this travesty of a marriage?

It was supposed to be a business arrangement so that he could eventually get his hands on Greywood Hall, though she was the one who'd complicated it by getting personal.

"He does what he's asked to do." Luke's confirmation was cool.

"What else have you arranged?" Rhia wasn't sure if she really wanted to know though was striving to be at least a little polite as they awaited their meal.

"I've arranged for a delivery of equipment from my London Office. I take it you have a bedroom I could use?" His manner was abrupt.

"In my cottage?"

It sounded like he was going to rearrange everything in her humble abode. Picturing him in her small sitting room and kitchen was bad enough. "What are you planning to do in my cottage?"

"Tonight I'm booked in here but tomorrow I plan to move in with you, although I know it's going to be a challenge because it's so cramped."

"This is my home you're whinging about. You've no right to talk about it in such a condescending way. It may not be a huge mansion, but it's where I live." She felt trapped even more.

The waiter arrived with their superbly presented entrees. Rhia was too edgy to even taste hers, though Luke proceeded to clear his plate as he picked up the conversation.

"That's not what I meant. I run a huge operation, and I have some computers running concurrently, hence the need for space. I'll limit as much as possible while we're in your cottage, since it will be only for a few days. You do have somewhere I can use?"

"If we aren't getting married for twelve days, why do you need to move in to my cottage tomorrow? Why not wait till we can move into Greywood Hall, then you'd have all the space you could ever need?"

With precision Luke placed his cutlery at the edge of his plate and explained that he'd contacted Miss Greywood's lawyer. Under the unusual circumstances, a complete renovation to Greywood Hall could be initiated without delay, though only if the cohabiting also began concurrently – with the acknowledgment that the officiating of their marriage would follow in due course since the registrar was already organised and documentation was in order.

He'd still be moving in tomorrow? Even if they didn't marry right away? Rhia was proud of the businesslike tone she managed to employ.

"You're desperate to start tomorrow so that the year will be completed sooner?"

"Not exactly how I was thinking Rhia."

She ignored his teasing. "And the residence qualification? Did the lawyer clarify how often you'd need to be home?"

"He did." His answer was brusque as he scanned the dining room.

"And?"

His gaze slid back to lock onto hers. He parroted. "It would seem that I must be in residence with you for the whole duration, initially in your cottage and soon at Greywood Hall. You must accompany me if I have to be away from Greywood Hall for more than one night for any business or pleasure visits abroad, or elsewhere in the UK. If the two of us are away for longer, except with prior authorisation, the visits can be for no more than one week."

"In other words we're literally joined at the hip?"

Rhia's jaw dropped, unable to prevent her noisy gasp. A waiter hovering to collect their plates perked up his ears at her comment. His slight twitch indicated he had heard it, and she was embarrassed.

"A nice way of putting it, Rhia," Luke murmured not in the least put out. In fact he seemed amused.

"What if you have to be away and it isn't convenient for my work schedule?" she asked, going off on a tangent.

"Rhia, I know what you do for a living." Luke's tone was frustrated. "You're a historian, currently a researcher of family history. I know perfectly well that you can work almost anywhere if you've got internet access and courier services. You'll manage."

"That's very kind of you." She didn't try to stop her words from sounding waspish. "For your information sometimes I do have to be away from home looking at original sources which can't easily be sent as copies. What happens then? Do you have to follow me around the country?"

"No." Luke's admission was reluctant as though not happy to be put on the spot. "I'm the one who has to be in residence most of the time."

"So I could be away without you and still meet the legal requirements?" Rhia was feeling marginally cheered.

"I'd have to clarify that again with the lawyer, though I imagine it could only be for the same short periods of time as stipulated for me."

Going off gallivanting suddenly sounded quite appealing to Rhia, though Luke's scowl indicated he didn't care much for that idea. "Maybe this won't be so bad then if I needn't have to be shackled to your company all the time." She truly brightened for the first time that day. "I do like to get away from time to time."

Luke was riled. "Remember we have our signed contract, Rhia. I'm your only lover and you're my only lover."

"I wasn't necessarily meaning I'd go off somewhere and have mindless sex with some one night stand, or some passing acquaintance, Luke. I merely meant we'd not have to be quite so much in each other's pockets."

The waiter happened to place their main courses down just at that moment. His mouth twitched, his eyes hard put not to show his amusement at the interesting statements being made by them. Rhia stuttered a little to clarify for Luke, her answer blithe.

"Except, it just so happens, I like living in this part of the world. I moved here by choice a year ago so I probably won't be away from home too much."

An edgy silence followed till Rhia felt she'd scream with the agony of it. Doggedly she picked up the threads of her conversation. "What else?"

"What do you mean what else?"

"What else have you organised already?" She grabbed up her knife and fork and stabbed the first thing she could find on her plate.

Luke exhaled as though any conversation was a trial for him now. "You may already have heard some activity at Greywood?"

She nodded her tone still challenging. "You're certainly right about that. They woke me up far too early this morning."

"Sorry," Luke continued not really sounding contrite. "That was the scaffolding arriving. We start early to maximize the daylight hours."

"Of course, never waste a minute," she scorned. She was beginning to think that should be his nickname.

"You're right; I don't like wasted time." He sounded very irritated by her censure yet resumed the conversation. "Teams of craftsmen are starting roof and exterior stonework repairs at Greywood Hall at first light tomorrow. Other teams will be going inside to finalise the assessment of any interior damage so that work on internal renovations can begin as soon as possible, once I evaluate their findings."

He mechanically cut up his salmon and popped a bit in his mouth, now unruffled. Five minutes later he was still outlining the more long term plans he'd already instigated for Greywood Hall.

"You've arranged all this so soon?" Rhia was astonished. She'd moped around for the past twenty four hours daydreaming, wondering what the hell she'd got herself into, and he'd been organising goodness knows what.

"Rhia, it's my job." Luke smiled, for the first time a truly natural smile.

It whacked her in the gut!

"But it's impossible to get craftsmen to do even small repairs immediately unless it's a major catastrophe. How did you manage it?" She was impressed by his information, unable to maintain a stiff attitude.

Luke grinned. Her tension eased a little more. They continued to eat, their mouthfuls interspersed with sips of water alternating with the delicious crisp white wine he'd ordered.

"One advantage of having a lot of money is to pay people to do what you want, when you want. I have an army of highly skilled workers at my beck and call. If they have to be away from their home base for short durations, they know their pay will be generous, covering any inconvenience caused."

"Greywood Hall is a large property. It's going to take lots of people forever to restore it if you do it properly."

"Properly? What do you mean?"

"Renovations need to be thoroughly planned and not rushed. You mustn't spoil the character of it, Luke."

Not in the least put out by her doubtful tone, he smiled. "For the last five years I've been doing major renovations on English properties: most of them sites of some historical significance. I assure you I won't be rushing in and wrecking the character or the ambience of the place."

"It's got a lot of dignity, even if it is run down." Wistful images made her eyes glisten.

"Have you ever been inside?"

"No, of course I haven't."

His hand reached across the table and gently clasped her fingers. "Would you like to?"

His light touch was a balm. She managed to say that she'd love to see inside.

"Well, since we're not going for a wedding dress, we'll look over Greywood Hall this afternoon."

His thumb idly caressed her palm.

Whether it was the wine or something else that mellowed her, Rhia wasn't questioning: she felt much better than earlier and let the feelings flow. She listened to him explain that locating the keys the day before had been a tedious priority.

She sank back from the table, removed his hand from hers, and stretched her legs underneath, her toe inadvertently nudging his in the process.

When Luke purposely shifted his foot closer to her, a flush spread over her cheeks that she couldn't do a damned thing about.

He went on to detail other processes he'd already put in place, arrangements for him to move his main operations from London to Greywood Hall, telling her briefly about things he'd delegated to his capable teams of employees.

"But how can you just up and leave your work base, and still maintain your business?" She was amazed at how easy he made it all sound.

Luke explained how he always had support teams at a new project venue, so setting up at Greywood Hall was not much different from other situations, and he explained about the delegation processes he put in place when he travelled.

"If that's what you normally do, why can't you set up a temporary office at Greywood? You'd surely find a bigger space than my spare room?"

"There are too many distractions, and it's too easy to disturb me when I'm on the premises. I'll hold meetings up at the Hall, though I need the distance to get on with other work, since Greywood is only one of the projects I'm working on. Your room will be ideal."

They finished their meal, Rhia realising that her earlier fears about being with a rich man like Luke had been largely unfounded. When all was said and done he was just a man…well maybe not just a man. She'd never met anyone quite like him before.

For all they'd been at loggerheads, she'd felt something blossoming between them. By the time they left the restaurant, she was seriously impressed by the plans he'd already put into place for Greywood Hall.

"I'll follow you back in my own car, Rhia."

A short while later Luke's Ferrari drove through the main gates of Greywood Hall. Thor panted in the small rear seat, his tail swished, and his muzzle was squashed against the now drool washed windowpane. The hound's breathing was the laboured type of wheezing that dogs exhibit when they can't wait any longer for something to happen.

Thor wasn't the only excitable one in the car. The accord at the end of their meal was still in force, but now Rhia was also gripped with anticipation. Anticipation about viewing Greywood Hall, and anticipation about the future she'd signed herself up for.

"Where are all those noisy vehicles that woke me up this morning?" There was now no evidence of them on the driveway. Some had to have been delivery trucks.

"They'll not be back till tomorrow morning," Luke said. "My team completed the initial assessments before noon today. They'll be dashing out their proposals right now, so that they've got some down time tonight before another early start tomorrow."

"Ah! I'll set my alarm for five thirty then?" she laughed at Luke's marginal apology as she teased.

"More like five. Depending on how long it takes you to shower."

He wasn't joking about the time scale. Her mirth vanished in mock dismay.

"Are you telling me those trucks really will be there before six o'clock?"

Luke chuckled at her pretended indignation. "It's summer time. Dawn is hours before six, and some of the haulage companies work a twenty-four hour day. I'm expecting deliveries throughout the night."

"Overnight?"

Luke resumed as though she hadn't interrupted at all, his smile wide, his expression intended to placate. "Those trucks shouldn't bother you tonight. They'll be going through the back entrance. They'll approach Greywood from the opposite direction, and use that access to unload roofing materials in the stable courtyard. My technical team, however, won't arrive till after six at the earliest."

"Where are they going to arrive from if they're getting here so early?"

She already knew from his update at lunchtime many of the team had been flown up north the day before from various locations scattered across the south of England.

Luke named a hotel in the nearest town.

"Your squad doesn't get the same luxury as you?"

There was a whimsical twitch at his lips. "Usually my team and I do have the same accommodation, Rhia. It makes good business sense to be housed in the same place so that any meetings can be carried on, or concluded when convenient."

"So why is it different this time?"

"I didn't think you'd appreciate waking up the day after our wedding knowing that my team was roomed all along the same corridor."

"Oh!"

Mortification glowed as the implications of what he'd just told her sank in.

She'd wrecked all of his careful plans with her confrontational attitude, refusing to have the ceremony the next day. He'd planned it so that the two of them could be more private, staying away from his team regardless of the inconvenience it would cause to his business requirements.

Although quite chagrined by it all, there was no way she would back down on agreements they'd already reached. She latched onto a different topic as the powerful car growled up to the house.

"This avenue of shrubs won't take too much to restore to full splendour."

They swept up towards the now overgrown turning circle to the side of the main house, a wide loop that would have originally been for a coach and horses. The travellers would have spilled out of the coaches beside the archway that led round the back to the stable block. From the archway, the honoured guests would have walked up the few steps to the main terrace and the imposing front porch.

"Are you a gardener?" Luke avoided the worst of the potholes and debris that littered the long disused turning circle. Though focused on the terrain, he kept the conversation going. "Are you personally responsible for that riot of colour in your back garden?" He flicked a swift glance her way. "I hadn't considered that you might do all the garden maintenance yourself."

"When I was little, I learned a lot from my grandfather. He had a large garden. I'd plant seeds during my Easter holiday visits then I'd always be delighted with what had magically grown when I returned for my school summer holidays. Naturally I'd no inkling of how much work went into the growing in between times."

"Though over the years you learned that magic has to be worked at and encouraged, didn't you?" He brought the car to a halt and killed the engine.

"Oh, yes. I was taught to do the hard graft as well. My fingers got very dirty."

"Would you recognise other plants in this garden?"

"Quite a lot actually."

"You're very confident." He grabbed a small backpack from the rear seat and then slung it across his shoulder. "Wait till I open the door," he cautioned. "I'll check what the surface is like for those devastating heels. I don't want you to break an ankle just getting out of the car."

Rhia accepted his hand out, mindful of where to place her feet. There was fleeting regret when he let her fingers loose to release Thor from the rear. The huge dog bounded out and made off down the stretch of lawn, as usual treating it as his own playground.

"I should admit at this point that I've had a lot more opportunities than you to find out what's in this garden. When I've walked Thor here, I've identified a lot of the plantings. Others I've looked up when I've gone home just because it annoys me not to be able to name them."

"Well now, there's another advantage to you having been here before. You can find out why I was willed Greywood, you can research the house, and you can also get yourself involved in the garden restoration."

Luke seemed increasingly satisfied with the idea she should get some pleasure out of helping to restore the whole property, not just the house itself during their contracted year. The appeal was mounting for Rhia.

"I'd love to." She looked around at the overgrown wilderness that was meant to be formal borders and edging for the wide sweep of unkempt lawn. "It's been easy to imagine what this garden was like, though many parts of the estate are severely choked with serious weeds and would need lots of effort to restore. Too much for one person."

Rhia caught Luke's gleam of amusement, in his eyes and in his soft chuckle. "Ah. Silly me." She giggled at his humour. "I guess you're planning on an army of gardeners?"

"Whatever it will take to get it in shape. And if that's a huge team – so be it."

His arm snaked around her shoulders, holding her in a light grasp as he turned her and pointed to the walled garden. She was so close to him an involuntary shiver rippled.

"So, what would you do with that?"

"From the contours that are still discernible, the walled kitchen garden over there I believe was most likely re-planted in Victorian times." She couldn't help but remember spying on him from the walled garden a few days before; her first sight of him. Swallowing a little, she concentrated on answering him. "It's a total nightmare actually, though it would be a magnificent project to undertake its restoration. The scale of it could comfortably feed and flower the whole house, which was what it was designed for, of course."

"What would you do with this terrace?" Luke turned her around a little, his arms hanging loosely over her shoulders. Again, there was a little frisson of awareness.

She answered quickly. "It needs complete repaving, but that needs to be solicitously done and as close to the original stone as possible."

"Why do you say that?" Luke's chin perched comfortably on the top of her head, his breathing irregular.

"It's obvious." She thought he was serious till she felt the twitch of his lips as he grinned. "The paving matches the stonework of the walls so it's natural that it needs replacing as close to the original as possible – though the originating quarry is unlikely to be still active."

"I couldn't agree more," he chuckled, and then moved away from her.

She guessed he mustn't like touching her, though she knew someone who did.

"Thor!" she bellowed. "Here, boy. Come here." The huge dog halted his gallop across the lawn and headed back towards her.

Rhia started off towards the central pillared entrance-porch, nestled between the bases of the curved forestairs, desperate to put space between them.

Luke grasped her hand before she'd taken two steps. "We're not using those doors."

Wrenching her fingers from his grasp her voice was wobbly. "Why not? Don't you have a key yet?"

From the backpack, he extracted the biggest iron key that she'd ever seen.

"This is the key, though that's not the problem, Rhia," he explained. "On the other side of those doors is the rudimentary security that Amelia Greywood must have ordered. She was a resourceful woman… or she had somebody else acting for her.”

“Well, come on.” Rhia urged affected by his humour. “You’re bursting to tell me.”

“There are three or four layers of the heaviest vestibule furniture blocking the doors – a basic barring of the door – to keep unwanted burglars out.”

“Didn’t keep you out though.” She grinned.

Luke grabbed her hand and towed her away to one of the exterior curved staircases. “Be careful with those heels. As you already know, the stairs are passable, but only just.”

He grasped her hand as they climbed up to the balcony and along to the centrally situated first level doors, Thor sniffing at their heels, unwilling to miss anything during this exciting adventure.

At the substantially glazed double-doors, Luke produced an immense chain of keys from the backpack. Each key had little colour-coded sticky labels indicating their use. Selecting one, he turned the key in the ornate metal lock. To her amazement, it almost made no sound at all, and the door glided open.

“How impressive!”

“That would be because I added a little oil yesterday,” Luke cleared his throat. He bowed in front of her. “Would you care for a guided tour of this magnificently elegant property, Miss Ashton?”

“I’d be delighted, Mr. Salieri.”

Rhia curtsied back, failing miserably in her attempt to hold out her tight straight skirt, making the hem ride up higher on her thighs. His gaze flickered as he focused on her momentarily exposed legs.

She was taken completely by surprise when he slid one arm around her shoulders, reached down with the other and tucked it under her legs, swinging her up in his hold as though she was marshmallow-light. He then stepped into the upper hallway. He cuddled her tight to his chest savouring her floral scent with a noisy sniff.

"Gorgeous."

"What are you doing? Put me down."

She was both delighted and embarrassed by the theatrical gesture.

"This is how you make a grand entrance into a magnificent property like this one will be."

Moments passed, his gaze totally focused on her. Surprising her, he snatched a quick kiss. "In the arms of your…" A second kiss lingered. "…only lover."

Luke released her gently to the floor.

"I'm sad to say this isn't the place for dallying. There's too much debris around here, Rhia. Much as kissing you again appeals, it isn't safe. One wrong step and you'll have a broken ankle."

Rhia looked down. The hallway was littered with potential hazards from the considerable damage caused by the leaking roof and ingress of rainwater near the now badly-fitting doors. Huge chunks of plaster coving cluttered the area.

"Okay. I believe you."

Luke carefully led her into the grand entrance hall, back to the business of being a tourist in the dilapidated house.

The first level entrance hall was a room of magnificent proportions with a two storey high ceiling dominated by a huge chandelier of dull metal and even duller dusty crystal.

"That will be absolutely marvellous after a good cleaning. It's beautifully fashioned."

His wry expression told her that he wasn't as certain as she was of the hidden beauty that lay deep beneath the grime.

"Thor!" Rhia called the dog to join them as they went exploring.

The first floor level, immediately above the ground floor, was a maze of formerly splendid reception rooms. Luke had explored them the previous day telling her he was delighted to find they were not in quite as bad shape as he'd originally suspected. The water damage from the leaking roof was largely confined to the attics and one end of the third floor. The large formal drawing room was in reasonable shape though furnishings were sparse. The smaller informal sitting room was the opposite. It was crammed with well-worn mismatched pieces.

"Wow. This is a very grand dining room."

Rhia's enthusiasm bubbled over even more when she entered the impressive long rectangular room. The elegantly decorated dining room was graced with a huge mahogany table set with more than a dozen matching chairs: a table that had been swept clean and which Rhia learned was being used by Luke as a temporary operations centre.

The room still had an enormous painting dominating the fireplace wall. Elaborately framed, it was an equestrian scene with a handsome young woman regally seated on a beautiful chestnut horse.

Rhia commented that though beautifully done it was disproportionate. Luke said he thought it looked quite pleasant but explained he was no expert of paintings.

"The woman and horse have been added to an original landscape, and their proportions are wrong," Rhia pointed out. "See here? These brush strokes have been over-painted by an amateur. The bucolic background, which has definitely been done by a much more skilled artist, is probably an image of what the estate looked like in former times. That practice of over-painting isn't actually all that uncommon."

"Why would someone do that?" Luke was intrigued as he inspected the areas she'd pointed out.

"Often it was because there was no new canvas to use. A prepared canvas of this size would have been pretty expensive for an amateur to have bought."

As she demonstrated her historical knowledge, they wandered around.

The sizeable library, an unusually bright room for the purpose, was well preserved. It had escaped most of the dampness and water damage that some of the other rooms had suffered from.

"This room has been well used." She was delighted with the contents in glazed cabinets and on the open shelving. "Oh, heavens. Look at these. These dog-eared books really have been read, unlike some country homes where the books were only showpieces."

"I know what you mean. Some of the properties I've renovated came with rooms partially furnished, and in a few cases, the stock in the library wasn't wanted at all by the departing owners. Like you say, never valued and rarely read."

They made their way steadily from room to room. Many of the rooms indicated treasures had already been removed. Faded wallpaper with obvious outline marks where paintings and wall hangings had been were evidence of this. Some rooms were minimally furnished and the furniture that had been left had been spread around, leaving an eclectic if mismatched décor. The condition of the items was fairly poor – not water damaged – just suffering from continuous use and sheer age.

Rhia's fervour bubbled over whenever she discovered something ancient or beautiful. The value of each individual piece was minimal, yet they were period pieces nonetheless. She shared her knowledge of antiques as they wandered.

"How come you recognise these so well?" Luke asked as she enthused over small marquetry card tables in the main salon.

"Antiques and old memorabilia are a hobby of mine. I factored in some specific furniture and architecture classes into my degree work at university. My grandmother had a few interesting bits and pieces. As a child I was fascinated, not by their value but by their anecdotal history. All of these pieces have a story behind them, whether a personal family account regarding the people who used them on a daily basis, or the history of the craftsmen who created them."

Luke was silent.

"Sorry. I didn't mean to bore you."

"Not in the least. This is the part that I always leave to other experts. When I renovate a property I call in the best people to restock with suitable period artefacts. I never ever entertained the notion that they might have an actual personal history. It's a fascinating thought." His grin widened, his expression quite delighted. "Now I know your expertise will be a godsend in interpreting and sorting through all this guff."

"Guff?" His particular vocabulary offended the historian in her, yet she knew he was teasing her.

"Guff." He laughed again, "Plenty of guff, and I can't get rid of one single bit till it's all investigated and you reveal the mystery."

"Luke Salieri. You're a total Philistine. Do you know that?"

The large family and superior guest bedrooms on the second floor, some with adjoining bathrooms and sitting rooms, were in reasonable condition, structurally speaking, though very dated.

Luke explained he was glad that the furnishings on the first and second floors would be able to be renovated, not because they would be worth more money to him but because they could be used in the future.

Thor's sudden lively barking made them descend to the ground floor. They investigated the kitchen area, Rhia hoping against hope that the dog wasn't ferreting after some small livestock – like mice. They found him sniffing and pacing at the back door, which led out to the stable yard.

She realised he was giving them notice of his needs. "Sorry, boy." Gurgling into his coat, she hugged him. "Too well toilet trained now, aren't we?"

Luke unlocked the door and let the hound flash outside. "I'm very glad to hear he's well trained. Think of the places he could leave a little parcel inside this enormous house."

The kitchen cupboards were full of items from varying time periods, from pre-Victorian through to the 1950s and '60s. It was a treasure trove of historical artefacts which made a wonderful collection.

"These ground floor rooms are almost perfect for opening to the public." Rhia laughed in delight.

Having opened a cupboard door she added, "The house is stuck in a time warp."

"You're saying that and you haven't seen the third floor or the attics yet," Luke warned. "Next place on our tour, Miss Ashton."

Finding a suitable enamel bowl, Rhia filled it with some water for Thor who gambolled outside the kitchen door, overheated from the warm house and his enthusiastic bouncing around. Setting the bowl in the shade of an outhouse, she tethered Thor's leash and ordered him to stay there for their return.

Investigating the third floor and the attics was next.

"I first saw you from this bedroom window," Luke said, his voice whisper soft. "You and Thor came out of the woods. You looked like a little woodland sprite."

"Me a sprite? Some folks I know would call me more of a bad-tempered imp."

"That autumn coloured suit you're wearing today makes you look even more like a woodland nymph." His arms snaked around her waist, his chin resting on her shoulder. He hugged her in a loose grasp as they looked out at the scene below.

She rather liked the warmth.

"Let's see what the historian in you will make of the rest of this floor."

Chapter Seven

"This is so fantastic!"

Luke trailed after Rhia as she wandered around the nursery bedrooms, watched her fingers gently swing the Victorian crib and listened as she described some of the more obvious decorative artefacts that still littered the rooms.

He appreciated her chuckles of merriment as she squeezed herself onto the built in seat of the desk in the schoolroom and lifted the angled wooden lid, something he'd not thought to do a few days before. Her eyes twinkled enthusiastically as she rummaged around the surprisingly still cluttered inside and pulled out a small book.

He was coming to the conclusion that he'd like to do an awful lot more silent observation of this captivating woman.

"Oh, my goodness," she squeaked. "This is incredible, Luke. This might even be one of the very first editions of this book."

Luke leaned closer to read the title of the gold tooled burgundy leather bound volume. "A Child's Garden of Verses. R. L. Stevenson."

Opening the inside cover, Rhia read aloud, "23rd May 1896. To Jo-Jo on your eighth birthday from your Aunt Maria."

Her voice hitched as she continued with the inscription written in flowery copperplate writing which she held up for him to see. "Get well poppet, for the world needs to see your cheerful smile."

Her eyes glistened as she twisted around to look up at him. At first he thought they were emotional tears before her gleeful smile almost knocked him out.

"Look at the postscript." Her laughter bubbled over as she shared the book with him, pointing to the area of the page that caused such mirth.

His arms bracketed around her as he finished the oral read. "And don't climb any more trees. Young ladies do not ever have broken legs – it's not dignified."

There was a further post-postscript that they read out together. "Check page 83" They flipped the pages till they came to the relevant one. The poem they found was titled Good and Bad Children.

"Children, you are very little,
And your bones are very brittle
If you would grow great and stately,
You must try to walk sedately."

Luke thought the rest of the poem didn't seem particularly relevant to Jo-Jo's predicament, though the message from Aunt Maria was very clear.

"Maybe you can find out who Jo-Jo was?"

"I'm sure I can," Rhia's response was confident. "Eventually. Do you realise that there's a museum full of stuff here, Luke."

"Are you telling me you're already angling for an assistant?" he chided.

"No bloody way!" The denial was vehement her husky laugh reaching parts inside him he didn't know existed. "This is my project, Sonny Boy. You've given it to me, and you'd better believe I can manage."

Luke didn't doubt it. He didn't doubt she'd manage it for one minute. He already knew the little sprite of the woods had a tenacious streak a mile wide.

It was definitely time to call a halt on the bedrooms floor; the dusty old beds just too close for comfort. He led her away from the temptations of the third level, ascending an extremely narrow little staircase in the centre of the house which led to the attic.

Rhia was nothing like any of his previous girlfriends. Her confrontational attitude was balanced by a dry humour he was beginning to appreciate, and she was definitely entertaining. Not easy to be around, yet, though he had a feeling that would change in time.

Perhaps he could manage to keep a relationship going with her for longer than a few weeks. That would be a real achievement for him given his past record, though it was evident that Greywood Hall would keep her actively employed for a long time to come.

"Oh, jeeze." Rhia's exclamation came when they reached the attic floor. "It's so gloomy up here. And this is what it's like on a sunny summer day. Can you imagine how awful this must have been during a freezing dark winter?"

It was just as well she was excited by their explorations of the amazingly dusty and smelly attics because the leaks in the roof were all too evident on one side of the house and they were what drew more of his attention. The deteriorated wood was fetid in places, to be avoided in others as it looked unsafe.

The attic staircase led onto a narrow panelled corridor that ran the length of the whole house at the back. Although it had walls, it didn't have a ceiling as such: most of it lay open to the rafters. There were a few tiny windows which provided a little natural light – though not much since they were cobweb meshed. It must have been a dismal prospect for the army of servants who would have been housed up there.

Luke didn't need Rhia's input to tell him that in Victorian times the female servants were likely to have been quartered in the attics – well away from the horny male servants who were more than likely housed on the sub-ground floor, if they ranked senior enough and lucky to be inside. The other males would have been quartered in the outbuildings – the abode of the lower ranks.

At each opposite end of the long attic corridor, alongside the cold exterior side walls of the house, lay six small domestic servants' bedrooms accessed from another little passage that lay across the breadth of the house. So twelve of them in all – tiny cubicles barely bigger than cupboards that were minimally and poorly furnished. Each still held a narrow wooden cot, a very small wooden dresser, and a series of iron hooks on one wall. That was it.

There were no bathrooms on the attic floor, not even a privy of any kind: the chamber pot ruled.

"After a hard day's fourteen or sixteen hours of sheer toil what did the servant have to look forward to?" Rhia asked as they wandered along the seriously damaged end. "How heavenly it was to be up here, at the top of the house, nearer to her God."

Her sigh was dramatic. "Imagine the parlour maid just dying for her thin mattress of straw with a tick cover, a scratchy woollen blanket, and these simple, wood panelled walls."

Luke laughed at the description because she was covering empathy with sarcastic humour. "Yes, and I'm sure some of them did really die up here of illness, loneliness and old age." He had been around old mansion houses long enough to know some of the sad parts of their history.

The four main storage rooms were huge in comparison. Taking up the rest of the attic space, they were completely open to the wooden joists and roof trusses. They were stuffed with discarded furniture, trunks and cases, earliest bicycles, toys and other memorabilia.

"There's weeks of work just in this attic storage alone, Luke. It goes back centuries." Rhia almost danced a jig in excitement. "Although some of it's damaged beyond repair there's still plenty that can be restored."

Even he could see that the Greywood family had been natural hoarders. By the time they descended to the ground floor, he was surprised to find they'd spent over three hours investigating the premises. Thor was pacing: hunger driven.

Witnessing Rhia's professional enthusiasm, he'd had to keep reminding himself she wasn't a dalliance – he was using her in a completely different category – for a whole year.

He had no words to describe the situation he'd got them both into.

They got back into the confines of his car and drove the short stretch to her cottage. He climbed out to open her door and pecked her cheek before he released her. "I'll be here at your doorstep just before nine o'clock tomorrow morning. My office materials are being delivered around then."

****

Rhia spent the evening hours in a frenzy of sorting out the only spare room that she had. Upstairs in her little cottage there were three bedrooms and one bathroom. Her own bedroom wasn't the largest, though it had the best view over the countryside. The fully-furnished guest bedroom was the biggest of the three, and the third she used as an unfurnished storage room for her historical paperwork, packed away in stacking plastic crates.

Deciding that she'd be best to have the largest room empty, she moved all the furnishings from the guest bedroom into the smallest room. By the time she'd rearranged everything to her satisfaction, and had scoffed a light meal, exhaustion had descended. At ten o'clock, she flopped into bed and fell fast asleep to awaken at around three a.m. It was just after six when the traffic making its way to Greywood Hall started up again.

By then, there was no point in trying to sleep. Feeling groggy, she got up yet contrarily her body was also hyper with nervous energy. Luke was going to move into her little cottage. It was recklessly insane. She hardly knew the man.

She spent far longer in the shower than she normally did, pampering herself just a bit more thoroughly.

Luke arrived and took over Rhia's life.

"Come up and see if what I've cleared will be enough space, although if it's not good enough there's really not much more I can do about it."

She wasn't quite sure how to play it because he was so distant, as though regretting the situation. He'd simply said good morning to hcr and was avoiding eye contact – but he was the one who was invading her life, so why should she do all the accommodating? She decided to play it cool. After all, she'd be getting a whole year's worth of mega-interesting work out of the deal, if he stood by the contract that she'd already signed. He didn't need to be friendly or even like her at all for that.

Upstairs Luke bypassed her bedroom with barely a glance when she pointed it out. He spent even less time looking at what was now her spare guest bedroom before he went into the room she'd cleared.

"It's fine. My crew might need to do a little rewiring, though they won't make any mess."

His answer was abrupt. Adding a brief appreciation of her efforts in clearing the place, he then high-tailed it back downstairs and went straight outside, barely acknowledging her trailing presence behind him. Spending time in the garden getting acquainted with Thor was obviously his plan, so she left him to it.

She was still miffed when the doorbell pealed a short while later, heralding the delivery van, and left it to Luke. Focusing on the work in front of her, she ignored the footfalls above her and his terse instructions to his men. She only acknowledged a disturbance when his head and shoulders popped in the sitting room door. The smile on his face was forced.

Not in the least missed by her.

"I'm taking a quick nip along to Greywood to check on the roofing materials. I'll be back in an hour or so when the guys here should be through."

"Do what you like!" She let her mutinous face show exactly how she felt about his offhand attitude.

"Rhia." Grasping her hands from her keyboard Luke pulled her to her feet. "Believe me. I'm not pissed off at you; just frustrated by some events."

Her scoff belied his words. "You could have fooled me."

One of his crew loped noisily down the stairs calling Luke's name.

"See you later."

He was gone before she could draw breath. Rhia could make neither head nor tail of this man that she'd agreed to marry.

A while later the efficient crew had fully installed everything. The furnishings, the telephone systems, computers and peripherals were up and functioning where Luke had ordered them. He'd already been back for more than thirty minutes and was chomping at the bit. Rhia had no doubt about his agitation because it was coming off him in waves. He'd been up and down the stairs so often she thought he must have worn out his shoe leather by now, popping his head into the sitting room to give her unnecessary updates and disturbing her pathetic concentration yet again.

Perfunctorily thanking the men, she heard Luke close the front door before he hurried in once again to speak to her.

"I've ordered a catered lunch for the crew up at the house. I'm already late for an arranged meeting, but if you want to come up later and eat there will be plenty. Otherwise, I'll call in the evening and let you know when I'm finished with the initial assessments of Greywood."

He was off before she even finished saying goodbye. She was learning he was very good at that.

During the course of the afternoon, the sounds of Luke's helicopter flying in and out a number of times disturbed her after a solitary lunch. It was ferrying men and materials back and forth, Luke having established that one of the back fields was a suitable landing space. She wanted to be in the thick of things, along at Greywood making a start to her investigations, but Luke hadn't invited her. He hadn't even hinted that she should start that afternoon. In fact, his swift exit had indicated he probably didn't even want her anywhere around him at all.

By seven that evening she hadn't heard a cheep. Peeved by the lack of contact, and very nosy about how things were progressing, walking Thor gave her the perfect excuse to head to Greywood. It was too tempting not to use the main entrance and front drive to enter the property. The gates now permanently open, she walked up the long rhododendron sweep with no thoughts of trespassing or guilt. Well, maybe a little guilt still remained, though Thor pranced about normally enjoying what he had come to think of as his territory anyway.

***

Up in the dining room, Luke rose from his chair when he heard Thor barking. If the wolfhound was down there, then so was Rhia. He told himself lots of things to justify why he was inordinately pleased she'd come to him.

Moving away from the long mahogany table, he couldn't resist looking out into the garden to watch her approach. Thor bounded around her. She was just a woman and Thor was just a dog, so why was he so happy to have them disturb him? Usually, he'd be so focused that very little would break his concentration, but he was honest enough with himself to acknowledge it had been shot that afternoon. The tension that still beset him had only a little to do with the complexities of the new project of restoring Greywood Hall and more to do with his move to Yorkshire and more specifically into Rhia's cottage. He had never lived with any of his former girlfriends, his work taking him from home so often it would have made cohabiting very impractical. Now, he was going to have to share a domestic situation with Rhia for a whole year, the woman who was right down below the window now playing the fetching games Thor loved.

Luke realised he'd completely lost track of what the assembled group were discussing.

"We've done enough for today, guys," he declared as he turned back to the table. "It's already well past seven o'clock. We'll resume our findings tomorrow morning." For all of them it had already been a long day; a very early start, his team more than happy to wind up their discussions. "We'll meet at nine tomorrow, here in the dining room."

A hasty shuffling of paper accompanied happy mutters of where the men intended to eat that night as they filed out of the room, Luke trailing in their wake.

He paused at the top of the forestairs watching Rhia as she stood down on the fringes of the lawn. She held tight to Thor's pelt and calmed him as the line of people picked their way down the crumbling staircases. Only after the last person had disappeared into the parked vehicles did she climb up to meet him.

Luke waited. "Hello, Rhia."

"I didn't come here to disturb you," she hastened to explain. "I just wanted to…" Her embarrassment was evident. "You didn't need to call a halt to your meeting because I arrived."

"We were winding up for the day anyway."

Reaching for her hand, he drew her into the hallway. Thor bounded in beside them not inclined to be left outside. His paws immediately skittered on the tiled floor surprising himself so much he dropped to his haunches, whining. Luke laughed at his antics.

Bending down to the dog, his tone was mock serious. "It serves you right, you silly hound. No gambolling inside the house."

He could have sworn Thor nodded his head in assent and for the rest of their short visit Thor remained glued to his side.

"You've got a conquest there," Rhia informed him. "You don't realise how wary he is of most people."

"My only conquest?"

"I'm not going to even think of answering that one," she laughed up at him, poking him with a sharp little fingertip.

"I just need to make sure I tidy up some of the paperwork. Then we can go."

She followed him into the dining room where he strode over to the enormous table that when fully extended probably sat at least thirty people. Closing down his laptop, he gathered up papers and blueprints and placed them into various containers and wallets. Within minutes, he held onto his laptop case with one hand, and tucked a filled document case under his elbow.

He skipped down the staircase like a nimble kid, followed by Thor who had tagged his every movement. At the bottom he paused and snagged Rhia's gaze.

"If you give me time to have a quick shower when we get back to your cottage, then we can go out somewhere for dinner?"

Rhia's shake of the head was quite firm. "Not tonight. I can rustle something up quickly."

They made it back to her cottage in record time, Thor delighted at the spanking pace they'd set, alternating between jogging and full out running. The hound was a little put out, though, when he was immediately popped into his outside enclosure, and given food and water. He whined and fussed, though Rhia ignored him.

"You just get in my way when I'm cooking, you big lout!" Her laughter trilled as she gave Thor an extra pat. "I'll fetch you later."

Luke couldn't resist commenting after he followed her into the kitchen. "I guess I'd best not get in your way, either, since I'm already a big oaf."

A cheeky grin was all he got as a reply while Rhia pulled out bits and bobs of food from the fridge before one hand shooed him away. "You've got ten minutes, if you still want to take that shower. You'll find towels in the bathroom cupboard and help yourself to anything else you fancy."

Loping up the stairs, he kept what he fancied to himself.

"This stir fry is amazing, Rhia!" He complimented her cooking skills around a mouthful of delicious Japanese noodles some fifteen minutes later. They'd been discussing the first stages of repairs to Greywood Hall as she'd served up the meal like a professional chef.

In a lull in the conversation, he found her studying him intently. This wasn't very different from him since he'd found he was also constantly watching her.

"You don't need to answer, though I'm more than curious." He spoke into the silence, willing her to answer. "You're a beautiful woman, so how come you're living alone in the boondocks?"

"Let's just say that London no longer appealed. I had some failed relationships I preferred to distance myself from." Her disgust wasn't lost on Luke.

After more searching questions spanning the next few hours, he was aware of how easy it had been for her to agree to a contract that would affect her life for a whole year. She had no immediate family to factor into the equation. An only child, as he was himself, her divorced mother had died just before she'd gone to university at eighteen. Her father, still alive, had largely been out of the picture from her early teens. Contact with him was reduced to Christmas and birthday cards since she'd not bonded with his much younger second wife and her young half-siblings. From her nonchalant attitude, Luke could tell she didn't hate or dislike her father, she just had nothing in common with him.

Rhia had a bunch of friends, though most of them were still in the London area so their contact was sporadic. Again, not a factor she'd needed to accommodate. He realised how lucky he had been because many women would have had greater commitments.

The meal, followed by a couple of cups of coffee, was convivial but afterwards the situation became strained. It was well past ten when a tension descended and their easy talk dissipated. The spectre of bed loomed. When she insisted on tidying up the kitchen herself, he didn't protest and instead took the easy way out saying he still wanted to do some more reading of the day's renovating proposals.

"I haven't had time to clear the desk in the sitting room, though it won't take a minute to make a space for you." Rhia turned away from the sink.

He blocked the door to prevent her exit. "Not necessary. I can read them anywhere. I could do with stretching out anyway."

Embarrassment laced her humour. "You'll not manage that on my two-seater couch."

"Were my suitcases delivered today?" He hadn't even thought to ask earlier.

He noticed she couldn't meet his gaze and instead focused on wiping the wok she'd used. "They're upstairs."

"Okay, that's great."

Thor removing himself from his bed in the corner, to snuffle around the back door, halted the conversation – the dog having been brought into the kitchen after Rhia had finished cooking the stir-fry.

"It's okay, boy. I'll let you out in a minute." Rhia dried her hands on a towel.

It had been years since Luke had been around dogs, but he didn't like the thought that she trailed the lanes so late. "Do you walk him far at this time of night?"

Her soft laugh was reassuring. "No. He gets his walks during the day and makes do in the garden before bedtime." Opening the back door, she followed Thor. "We won't be long."

"I'll head upstairs, then." Luke wasn't sure she heard him since she'd disappeared into the night dim.

Two suitcases were strategically placed just inside the door of the room Rhia had pointed out as now being her guest bedroom. He switched on the overhead light and peeked in. The room was small and simply furnished with a double bed covered with a fairly anodyne duvet in swirls of pale blues. Mirrored wall cupboards, along one wall, provided storage. He slid one open. A totally empty space faced him. Luke stared. It probably hadn't been clear the day before. He couldn't resist the temptation to sneak a peek in her bedroom. Evidence of her occupation was everywhere – cosmetics on the tops of cupboards, jewellery and other feminine things were scattered around. The room wasn't large but the space was made even smaller by the stack of transparent plastic crates in one corner, crammed full of books and paperwork.

She really had rearranged her life to accommodate his bizarre proposal, for the coming year, though it was significant that the crates were in her bedroom and not the other.

Back in the guest room, he pulled out his night-gear and headed off to the bathroom.

Her signature wasn't yet on the marriage certificate.

Chapter Eight

Rhia came to, wondering what on earth the clanking noise was.

It took no time at all to realise it was the sound of her shower running. Hearing someone else close by was so weird because she'd had few guests since moving in to the cottage. Pretending it wasn't happening unfortunately didn't work, but the creaky plumbing noises only lasted for a little bit longer. On checking the time, she groaned. It was only a little past five o'clock.

Turning over and burying her head under the pillow, she tried to will sleep to return. Luke might want to rise at that hour. She didn't. She had almost drifted off again when Thor's barking downstairs clinched the deal. Even though she knew it would do no good, she bawled at him to stop.

Her reply was even more excited barking.

"Thor! Would you just shut up? It's way too early for walkies!"

Belatedly, she remembered Luke. Struggling out of bed, she grappled with her dressing gown muttering that she didn't care two hoots if Thor treated Luke as an intruder. That thought made her mouth twist in a reluctant smile, yet before her arm was properly in the sleeve she realised Thor was now barking outdoors. From the window, she saw her beloved dog capering about with the man who now shared her house. He had found one of the dog's rope toys and was fast becoming great friends with her playful dog. Her mood wasn't improved by the sight. Strange resentment overflowed as she crept back into bed.

"You're welcome to him, Thor. Where's your devotion to me, then?"

As she closed her eyes again, the thought occurred that Luke had made it less traumatic by uncomplainingly sleeping in the spare room. She hadn't known how to play that particular scenario when she'd walked outside with Thor the previous night. She wasn't sure how to deal with it now either.

Still not particularly refreshed when she went downstairs, she saw that a sticky note decorated her table. It informed her that catering was again organised for lunch up at the hall for the squads working there and she was welcome to join them. He'd be back sometime later, though wasn't sure when.

Settling to do her research work wasn't easy, yet she ploughed on wanting to clear the decks of work she had to finish before anything could be started up at Greywood Hall.

It was after her lunch, a quick sandwich that she'd taken outside to eat, when Luke returned. Having exchanged a brief hello at the door, he disappeared upstairs to work, Rhia mentally noting that she'd need to get some spare keys. The sounds of him talking on the phone, and the buzzing of incoming calls was what now disturbed her concentration, so she took Thor for a long afternoon walk.

Strolling through the wood at Greywood Hall on their return, she was curious to know what was happening up at the house.

Already the estate teemed with workmen. Some were conspicuous clambering on the rooftops; other groups were examining the exterior of the building. Ladders and scaffolding were already everywhere, the men evidently assessing woodwork and stonework independently of each other.

She was so desperate to get her hands on all the Greywood treasures she almost breached their scaffold barricades.

Over on the main drive, she hailed a couple who were obviously discussing the plantings. "Hello! Are you here to assess the garden by any chance?"

The woman stared at Rhia before answering, as though reticent to reply before knowing who she was.

"My name's Rhia Ashton." She held her hand out in welcome.

The couple still looked undecided. After all, Rhia could have been anyone at all, especially wandering around dog walking.

"I'm going to be Mrs. Luke Salieri in a few days and just wondered how much of the garden you've seen already?"

The word Salieri was the magic key. After that, there was no holding the couple back. Bob and June Renton lived locally and were joint owners of a garden design service, with a team of gardeners in their employ. It was so relaxing to talk horticulture as they wandered around the grounds together before the Rentons declared they'd have to get back to their work base.

Thor wasn't so relaxed. He was confused. It was fine when he'd been in the wood where he could scurry around, but witnessing all the workmen in action seriously dented his territorial rights. Rhia kept him very close to heel curbing his tendency to bark when they got close to any of the workers. It was weird seeing so many people milling around what had been such a lonely and neglected old place. Only last week? It was so hard to credit it.

It was all happening so quickly. Luke had only known about Greywood Hall for five days. Though impressed by what a massive cash injection could do to change the state of affairs on the property, Rhia was astounded at how he could have all the relevant personnel on site so swiftly. How rich was this man she'd got entangled with? She wasn't interested in the amount of his wealth; she was merely overwhelmed by his financial flexibility.

Back at the cottage he paced around above her, his footfalls accompanied by the murmur of his voice. It wasn't any good. Rhia knew she couldn't possibly get any work done in the sitting room. Resolutely taking her laptop, knowing already that her internet router was efficient enough for outside coverage, she worked at her garden table, shading it as much as possible by lowering her parasol to the lowest level.

Thankfully the summer weather was still behaving, and it was pleasant to be outside. For the next couple of hours she tried to complete some work. Unfortunately, the least distraction broke her concentration, her thoughts immediately gravitating to the man in her upstairs bedroom.

The man whose voice she could hear through the open window conducting one phone call after another. How could Luke be immersed in his work when she could hardly string two sentences together? Sighing, she entered in another computer search and worked on till Luke appeared at the back door.

"So this is where you are?" His expression indicated delight, and though she couldn't be sure, maybe some relief? "When I saw the sitting room was empty, I thought you'd abandoned me."

"No. Just avoiding your pacing feet, Luke," she countered, her cynical smile drawing his gaze. "I thought my ceiling was going to collapse under your pounding treatment."

"You'll get a break now," he laughed. "I'm going along to Greywood for some briefings that I'm already late for, but we'll eat out tonight. Be ready to leave just before eight."

Later on, Rhia selected one of her best outfits since she'd no idea what location he had in mind.

"You look wonderful. Let's get going. I'm starved." His appreciative gaze matched his words.

She wasn't sure about the almost repeat of the previous evening. After an excellent meal and another genial conversation, she followed Thor outside on their return to the cottage.

Luke spoke from the back door. "I'll try not to disturb you. I've got more I want to check on tonight. See you tomorrow."

It seems he'd taken her hint quite well.

Rhia stifled a moan when her alarm sounded way too early at six o'clock. The house was silent. The spare bedroom door was closed though the office one was ajar, the room empty of Luke. Showered and dressed, she was laying a simple breakfast when Luke startled her by entering the kitchen.

"Good morning. I imagined you'd already gone since I didn't hear you upstairs," she said.

Long fingers slipped across his chin rasp, Luke still looking sleepy. "I'm normally up sharper than this, but I worked on till around two a.m."

"Can I get you anything?" She opted for an open question since she'd no idea of his breakfast eating habits.

"My usual is juice, coffee, cereal like you have here, and maybe a bit of toast. Any version of that would be great, though if you tell me where it's kept, I can fetch it."

Rhia grinned. "Sound good, since I'm not your servant." Pulling out a glass she demonstrated the cupboard contents. Opening the fridge she extracted the juice and pointed to the milk. Luke lifted the cartoon and opened the top. "Bowls up there, and the next cupboard has the choice of cereals."

In similar vein she prepared the filter, topped up the water and switched on the drip-coffee machine.

Nibbling at a piece of toast, she offered a tentative suggestion.

"I only have one small investigation to do to finish the current project I'm working on. That should take about an hour. I've nothing else pending that's in any way urgent so…" She determined to sound businesslike as she gathered their used cereal bowls and dumped them in the sink before sitting down again. "…how would you feel about me using my time at Greywood Hall? I could initially catalogue the paperwork discovered, or I could make a start on an inventory?"

It was awkward to maintain eye contact, having been the one to broach the subject of her being along at Greywood Hall, since Luke was slow to answer. His hands reached across the table, his fingers twining with hers; the tingling reassuring.

"If you want to do something up at Greywood, I wouldn't say no to you using your research skills right away." He pulled her to her feet and walked her to the door, one arm across her shoulders. "Though before that, you're officially going onto the workforce."

"Oh, no! That's not what I meant at all." Rhia was aghast at the thought she might sound grasping for the money he'd promised as a salary. She squirmed in his hold.

"No. Please listen." Luke's earnest gaze searched for her compliance. "If you're officially at Greywood, it means you can be factored in to the safety record of the building. My safety officer, Mike, always needs to know which personnel are present in the building, where they're working, so that any messy repairs, or even demolition, can be safely done with everyone accounted for and wearing any necessary equipment."

"Oh, sorry. I didn't realise. Forget I asked." Rhia backed off from her suggestion, backed off from Luke too as he released her stiff torso.

"It's just normal business practice." His tone was professional. "Your idea's magic, but I'd want you to be safe at all times. I can arrange to bring you on board this morning. I'll only need a few national insurance details just now and in a while your signature in a few places."

"If you're sure?"

"I haven't asked you to sign on yet since I thought you still had other clients' work to finish. Though if you're free, then there's no need to delay." A grin appeared, his eyes a soulful plea. "You know exactly how keen I am to get you started on the search for why Amelia chose me."

Up in the makeshift office a couple of hours later, Rhia was signing the few documents Luke had printed out, and was giving him the last of the information he needed when the doorbell pealed. She looked at her watch, an untameable grin widening. "That has to be Gus."

She was aware of Luke striding after her as she nipped down the stairs.

Gus did his usual, bear-hugging her after she opened the door. She returned the cuddle before introducing Luke.

The men shook hands, Gus' dwarf-like grin of welcome disappearing fast. She glanced at Luke wondering how to ward off what she guessed might happen next.

"You're Rhia's postman?" Luke's tone was cool but she was sure the dull flush hadn't been at his cheeks earlier.

"That's right young man. I may not be a relative of this young lady, but Rhia is as dear to me as any of my granddaughters who are dotted around this area. I may be seventy, but I can still appreciate how lovely she is and if you mess her about in any way, you'll have me to deal with."

Luke first reaction was amazement at Gus' words, followed quickly by a denial.

"I have no intention of 'messing' with Rhia."

Luke might have said more but when the phone rang upstairs, he made a quick exit muttering low Italian as he took the stairs two at a time.

Ten minutes later, and a lot of local gossip updated, Gus was gone. When she entered the sitting room, Rhia could hear Luke pacing above, his voice a muffle, immersed in work once again. The last research needed to complete her own current project was done quickly, after which she organised a new time schedule for completion of the two small client orders that still needed to be researched. A couple of hours during each of the next three mornings should be sufficient, allowing her to clear the rest of her time to investigate the contents of Greywood.

She itched to start because the thought that something important could slip through her grasp was taking on nightmare proportions. Luke needed to know why Amelia had bequeathed the property to him, yet the way his team had swooped in to do their initial assessments didn't make her feel at all secure about having plenty of time to investigate the contents of Greywood.

What if they boxed everything up and carted it off immediately? That thought horrified her! She didn't want one single thing moved, not even the broken bits in the attics. Nothing must be missed.

Pulling out two digital cameras and a video camera, she checked them all. Not good. None had been used for quite a while. Their battery power was too low, especially the video camera. Popping them into the chargers, she prepared to wait the short time necessary. The rest of her camera equipment, zoom lenses and portable tripod, were checked and set in the camera bag.

Mentally cataloguing, she went in search of some new notepads from the storage boxes upstairs, but the volume of Luke's voice wasn't in the least inspiring as she bypassed the temporary office.

"I don't bloody care what you have to do or say, Jeremy. I've told you before. Just don't ever pass over any more calls to me, do you understand, no calls at all."

Rhia was glad to nip back downstairs. If that was Luke in a temper, she never ever wanted to be at that end of his tongue. The pads and some pencils were popped into her camera bag. Ready. Now all she had to do was make sure what she planned would be agreed by her new employer.

"Luke?" she called up the stairs at lunchtime. "I've lunch ready down here if you want something to eat."

A few minutes later Luke entered the kitchen, plonked himself at her small table avoiding eye contact and fiddled with the cutlery she'd set out. She didn't know if his cool entrance was because she hadn't taken the food up to him…or what caused his mood, but it was definitely not pleasant.

"I wasn't expecting you to feed me lunch," he eventually stated, looking out of the window, his fingers tapping at the edge of the table.

Rhia wasn't quite sure how to handle his chilly tone but it rattled her composure. "It's nothing fancy. Just a lasagne I made last week and put in the freezer. All I had to do was re-heat it and toss some salad." Her nippy tone matched his fairly evenly. "You don't have to eat it if you'd rather go elsewhere." The local caterer was supplying daily to Luke's workers at the site.

"Some salad and lasagne would be just fine, please," he grunted so slowly she could almost hear the gritting of his teeth as he continued to avoid her eyes.

Was it sarcastic? Did he hate lasagne? Was he annoyed at having to come downstairs?

The atmosphere was so frosty she found she didn't care. There was no convivial conversation or attempts to touch her; Luke's mind was still wrapped elsewhere. Metaphorically biting her lip she served their lunch. A few awkward nibbles in to their meal, he swore vehemently in both Italian and English then slammed down his cutlery. He reached for her fingers and crushed them in his own, not enough to hurt yet enough for her to realise his frustration.

"Rhia, I'm sorry," he apologised stroking her palms gently. "Something came up this morning that put me in a really bad mood, though that's no excuse for taking it out on you."

"Apology accepted." Her tone was still brittle; however, she did relent sufficiently to add, "Forget it. Eat your lunch, please."

Afterwards they managed to converse better but underneath tension simmered a merry tune as Luke related some new developments. His tone was friendly enough – yet he was still in the grip of some pressure he wasn't talking about.

Although he was a man of many moods she hadn't yet seen all of them, not by a long chalk.

Would a year be long enough for that?

She wasn't at all sure since Luke still played lots of cards close to his chest. She would just mark up the present one to experience and act as though it didn't bother her.

"I'm heading for Greywood now," she informed him as he dried up the dishes she'd just washed, not expecting his help though pleased when he'd automatically done his share, even if a little awkwardly like a newbie at the job. "Is there any particular place you'd prefer me to start the investigations?"

"Not really," Luke methodically stacked the clean plates in her small cupboard. "What were you thinking of tackling?"

"I'm no professional photographer, but what I'd like to do first is take a good photographic record of what the place looks like just now. For cataloguing purposes," Rhia informed him, adding as an afterthought, "though maybe you've had someone do that already?"

"No. Nothing like that yet. My usual inventory team is busy elsewhere for the next few days." Luke then gave her some of his company's normal procedural background. "Cataloguing for historical purposes, for future use, has never really been a necessary part of my job. The properties I buy over don't need anything like Greywood will need."

"Don't any of your sites ever retain any of the original artefacts?"

Rhia was eager to know that answer because Luke had already mentioned in his past dealings some furniture and artefacts had been part of his original purchases. Her pulse spiked in alarm.

What was he going to do with the contents of Greywood? All she knew at the moment was that with her co-operation, regarding the marriage, he would end up as the owner of Greywood and its contents. She didn't know what would happen to it at the end of the all important year of occupation. The speed at which Luke implemented immediate repairs to the roofs told her that major changes were likely to happen to the interior before too long.

She didn't want to think of Greywood becoming a luxury hotel. She didn't want it to become a centre for team-building or corporate functions. Having only seen the inside just the once she already could hardly bear the thought that it wasn't going to rise like a phoenix and become a happy family home.

"Occasionally an artefact is used in one of the re-designed rooms," Luke told her as he completed putting the cutlery away.

Rhia forced her concentration back to his answer.

"My inventory team does a sweep in case any previous owner has made an oversight and might perhaps want to reclaim an item. They're usually accompanied by my interior decorators who decide whether an object might be suitable for a re-designed room, either in the original property or in another that we're developing." His gaze lingered on her. "Till I get all the permits for internal renovations at Greywood – they're being speeded through by the way – we'll concentrate on the roof repairs and on replacing damaged woodwork in the attics and third floor to make the building sound. Any other internal restructuring, or decorative work, will come later."

"Am I safe to wander around everywhere today?"

"It should be fine today, though make sure you check in with Mike when you arrive. He's in charge of safety. He'll issue your safety gear and tell you of any new developments as they occur." There was another searching gaze she couldn't interpret.

"Where will I find Mike?"

"He'll find you. I'll call to let him know you're arriving." Before he headed back upstairs to answer the constant calls, he added, "Make Thor bark when you arrive. Mike's bound to hear him and come down to meet you."

"That's no problem, Rhia. You've arrived just in time," Mike said, having greeted her at the first level doorway.

Mike, a rounded mid-to-late forties guy, smiled as he handed her a hard hat and a reflective jacket, showing her how to adjust them to size.

"Luke phoned about your plans. You're lucky we're not quite ready yet to start with the removal and renewing of the roof trusses on the damaged side. We'll need to clear the floor space before that happens…" Mike stopped on hearing Rhia's gasp of dismay.

"Oh, my God! Has anything been moved yet?" She was scared to ask because she didn't want to hear the answer was positive.

"Don't panic." Mike grinned, amused by her distress, his pale blue eyes twinkling. "Nothing's been moved yet. You'll be able to take all the photos you want, so long as it's today. Tomorrow's another story though, because we really do want to get into demolition mode on the roof tiles at the damaged end from first light."

"So you're saying I should start at the top of the house?"

"Good plan. Although you should be aware that some of the roofing guys will be wandering around assessing the inside woodwork more thoroughly in the attics, though they already know you'll be in the house and will work around you."

"Don't they need a clear space for that?"

"Not to inspect the woodwork itself." His deep voice was reassuring. "When you've finished photographing the whole attic floor, we'll get everything transferred to the non-damaged side. We'll use the empty attic bedrooms for storing the items and the two big areas on the better side if we need to. And if that's still not enough we'll move it down to the third floor."

Rhia's pulse settled to a steadier rhythm. So long as she had a good photographic record, she'd feel better about items being displaced…even temporarily.

Her digital cameras and video clicked constantly for the next few hours though she acknowledged the basic emergency lighting that had been installed by Luke's team for inspection reasons was inadequate for really good photographic quality. Still, it was sufficient for what she needed as she moved from area to area in the attics. Finished there, she worked her way down to the lower levels, Thor at her heels, still mystified by the comings and goings of workmen around the place.

Her video recording skills were pretty basic, but she made sure to still-capture with her digital cameras. Though she had never undertaken anything like this kind of job before, she had a historian's instinct for recording prime sources. She was meticulous in recording the order of the photographs, room by room, in her brand new notebooks.

The hours passed in an enthralled blur.

Though it was obvious that some expensive pieces of artwork had been removed from their hanging spaces, there were still many very old paintings and lithographs both on walls and set in frames that decorated tables and cabinets. They were a fascinating and time consuming study in themselves. Everything was, and she itched to start investigating.

The permanent grin that accompanied her, she couldn't prevent. She was so excited about the whole project, deeply honoured to be given the responsibility. In her current euphoric mood, she was thrilled to be legitimately wandering around Greywood Hall. Regardless of whatever happened during her cohabiting with Luke, she'd still have plenty of exciting work to do.

Somehow, only some parts of that reasoning pleased her.

As she toured, she noted the rooms which would require the bulk of her research time. The library in particular heaved with books and other paperwork. What had obviously been Amelia Greywood's bedroom suite had a small dressing room attached, which groaned with information. Inside a walk in closet in the dressing room, Rhia found boxes packed with facts relating to Amelia's activities, letters from friends and details relating to charity work and local organisations she'd been involved

with. There was a wealth of local history contained there –
months of study in them alone.

When she'd photographed every floor, she had just
enough time to venture back up to the attics. They were a
veritable treasure trove, and like a child in a sweet shop
she was desperate to investigate everything. There were
cartons and boxes of paperwork, larger chests holding
artefacts and clothing, discarded furniture and toys strewn
about.

Some portable cupboards and boxes could be
investigated in situ since they contained larger items but
others would be best removed downstairs for further
analysis. A particularly large cabin trunk looked so
enticing she couldn't wait to find out what it contained.
The ornate metal padlock dangled open, though the dust
on the lid indicated it hadn't been touched for many a year.
The top was just groaning free when strong muscled arms
reached around her and helped her lift it up.

Chapter Nine

"Let me help." Luke whispered the words at her ear as the lid popped open.

Rhia evidently hadn't heard his approach, his footsteps drowned out by the noise of the workmen on the outside of the roof nearby. Thor, now so used to his presence, hadn't even considered alerting her.

"I came to tell you that I'm meeting with the project leaders in the dining room in a few minutes. We'll likely run on till around seven thirty or eight." His tone he kept matter of fact: because being so close to her was unsettling.

"How about I make dinner for eight-thirty?"

"We could go out to eat?"

"I don't need to be taken out every night. I'm happy to cook for us if you can stand what I dish up."

"Okay. If you're sure."

Very domestic. Eating in was such a conjugal thing to do. He knew he'd best get used to it, but it was something he had always been rigorous about avoiding. Eating out gave out very different signals to the women he'd dated in the past. He had to concede though – the present situation was anything but normal. If he played houses with Rhia for a year, then they would have to do all these very domestic things a lot more often.

He reflected that one week ago the concept would have been farcical.

As he walked downstairs to his meeting, Luke's mind whirred. Would he be prepared 'do domestic' if he didn't find Rhia attractive? What if he'd only engaged her services in a paper marriage because she was a historian, to help him fulfil the conditions of the will and find out the historical mystery that dogged his heels? The thought of doing even basic domestic things with someone he wasn't attracted to now seemed a complete nightmare.

***

The next morning Rhia was stacking away their breakfast dishes when Luke loped back downstairs having only been up there for a matter of minutes. His face was like thunder again.

"I'm off to London to oversee meetings for other ongoing projects." His words were clipped, his manner distracted as though travelling was the last thing he wanted to do.

"Now? It's Saturday."

Rhia was amazed at the speed of his decision making, though she really shouldn't be since everything went at warp speed with Luke every day of the week.

"The helicopter is on its way, but I need to pop upstairs to check on a couple of things first."

His abrupt exit disappointed her, but he'd already rescheduled and reorganised a multitude of things to be at Greywood Hall during the previous few days. He left soon after saying his return would be late that night.

Realising their so-called wedding day was looming, Rhia took advantage of his absence. Before shopping for something suitable to wear, she arranged for a new set of cottage keys to be cut. A couple of hours later, having visited a number of boutiques and department stores in the nearest large city, she returned thrilled with the embroidered full-length sheath dress in white silk. Its vaguely Grecian design that bared one shoulder was perfect. She couldn't resist new lingerie that included a garter belt and white silky stockings. Her new shoes were high strappy heels that looked great. It wasn't a traditional wedding outfit but it was within her low budget, clung to her curves, and made her feel sexy. She didn't have a clue what Luke would wear but guessed he'd wear a formal suit of some kind.

Back at the cottage, she popped the items into her bedroom and settled down to process a digital record of Greywood Hall till Luke returned.

Unfortunately, it didn't quite work out as planned. By six that evening, he called to tell her his discussions were still not concluded and that he'd have to continue with the meetings the following day but would be back as soon as he could.

Rhia spent a lonely evening in her little cottage; something that she'd never felt before. Thor, although just as enthusiastic in his adoration, was unfortunately no substitute for Luke. Annoyed with herself, she couldn't deny that she missed him.

Luke returned the next day after lunchtime running Rhia to ground up in Amelia Greywood's bedroom closet where she had surrounded herself with an array of diaries and boxes of paperwork.

The house thronged with workers even though it was a Sunday, many of whom were already working on woodwork renovations in the damaged attic bedrooms, remodelling them to create larger, more spacious and user friendly accommodation. After brief hello, Luke took himself off to the cottage to resume his work.

Rhia purposely remained along at Greywood till after six o'clock and walked Thor home by a roundabout route as his last exercise of the evening. On her arrival, Luke insisted on going out that night for dinner to an expensive local restaurant. Glad that her wardrobe still held some classy items that she'd worn during her London days, she was spruced up in no time.

Dinner was wonderful.

If they had been dating, it would have been one of those 'I'm really getting to know you better' evenings. Tangling of feet under the table was inadvertent, yet thought provoking. The deep glances she was fielding from Luke were comfortable, though sometimes blatant.

Passing up on desert, they headed back to the cottage where they lingered a while over coffee before he declared more work awaited him. Collecting the cups, Rhia was unprepared for Luke's hands at her shoulders.

"I really enjoyed this evening, Rhia. You're a very easy person to dine with."

When he kissed her it didn't seem so much of a surprise. His lips didn't linger but the look did before he bid her goodnight. She was glad when he took himself off. With no real idea why, she still wasn't ready for the cohabiting as man and wife thing.

The next days were very similar except there were no more kisses. Admiring looks were quite often intercepted; but there was nothing physical. Luke managed to be disengaged and businesslike, able to compartmentalise his life much better than Rhia could.

It was as well that she was totally absorbed at Greywood for long hours.

"I've decided to renovate it as a completely domestic facility." Luke's words came as a surprise as they ate dinner in the cottage.

"No corporate re-styling at all?"

"None."

Luke's answer was curt as he looked out of the small kitchen window. She couldn't gauge how he felt about the decision, but he seemed tense, maybe even a little irritated about it. "I've researched the housing market in Northern England and it will be easier to sell off as a luxury domestic property when the year is up."

"Okay…" The thought of it being sold made Rhia cringe but that wasn't her business. "So, should I still carry on with the researching as planned?"

"Of course."

Rhia couldn't talk to him after that. She took refuge in clanking their plates into the sudsy water. She really wanted Greywood to be beautifully restored, but the thought of some unknown family living in it was gut wrenching. That part of the deal wasn't up to her though. She attacked the dishes more thoroughly than she needed, and her refusal of his offer to help was resolute.

"Since it's a lovely evening, I'm taking Thor out again when I'm finished here."

Her statement brooked no compromise making it sound like she didn't welcome company. Luke, who declared he still had plenty to work on that evening, didn't even seem to notice her bad mood.

The happy family living wasn't working quite so well. And they weren't even married yet.

Rhia focused on her researching but there was absolutely nothing perceptible pointing towards why Luke had inherited. None of the portraits indicated any likeness to previous Greywood males. The library research would be a huge undertaking and needed a lot of time. The diaries she'd found in the library and attics spanned a couple of centuries and would also take a long time to evaluate.

She decided her best bet would be to focus on Amelia's personal correspondence and paperwork and work back from there.

"Luke!" Rhia bounded up the stairs to the makeshift office the following day, clutching a few small photographs. "I've found it!"

"You have?" Luke completed his call, a huge grin on his face. He snatched her up and whirled her around the small space in the centre of the bedroom floor. "Why was it me?"

"Oh, no!" Rhia's chagrin was unmistakable. "I'm sorry…so sorry. I haven't found out why she named you. It's just that I was excited at finding these photographs of her that I dashed back to show you."

She rushed to lessen his disappointment. "You can now put a face to her. This one here?" She flashed a very small black and white Box Brownie type photo first. "This one is dated 1956 on the back. Read."

Luke read the spidery faded pencil writing. 'Left to right. Me, my mother Bethany and Julie Borthwick (her best friend) at Brighton pier.'

"This is what she looked like when she was thirty-eight."

"Thank you, Rhia. You're the greatest." Luke gave her a sound kiss as he held the photograph behind her. "I just knew you were the woman for the job. I've wanted to know what the damned woman looked like since I heard of her peculiar bequest."

Rhia was slightly flustered, yet inordinately pleased when he released her to devour the details in the photograph.

The kiss had been automatic on his part…and easily forgotten.

Amelia's strong boned face wasn't smiling, but she didn't look unhappy either. Her dark hair was clipped back from her face, a small pair of fancy winged glasses perched on her nose.

"Now look at these two." She was beside herself with excitement as she handed over more evidence. "These are even better; taken in 1988." Again there was writing on the back of the larger colour photographs. 'To Amelia. These are the best two photographs of the three of us at the Skipton County Fair, 1988. Best regards from Sophia and John Somerston.'

Amelia's face looked remarkably similar to the earlier one. Though the hairstyle was the same, her hair was a steel grey. The glasses were a different style, but she still had quite a strong set to her jaw. Rhia reckoned she'd been a forceful woman. Luke agreed.

Amelia had certainly been forceful enough to embroil Luke in their ongoing saga. She handed him all three photos. At least now, he could rant and rave at Amelia's photograph when he got fed up of his benefactress's little mystery which seemed impossible to solve.

"Make me copies." He handed them back. "If she keeps me in the dark too much longer, I might get frustrated and tear them up."

Rhia continued to immerse herself in cataloguing Amelia Greywood's personal memorabilia – a labour of love because it was truly fascinating to see how much had survived the decades. She'd found earlier photographs that she suspected were of Amelia as a younger woman, but couldn't yet find enough evidence to authenticate them. Nonetheless, there was a whole host of items which reflected Amelia's tastes and preferences.

In the attics, and in other cupboards, Rhia unearthed priceless items of clothing dating back more than 50 years. After very extensive searching of rooms, she found jewellery and ornaments which, though not hugely valuable, were an indication of the old lady's style. Her camera clicked constantly cataloguing everything. Her notebooks and computer spreadsheets filled up rapidly.

However, nothing in those searches pointed to why Luke had inherited.

At dinner she brought up the inheritance subject again. "What exactly did the lawyer tell you about the bequest?"

"What do you mean?"

Luke wasn't following her trail of thought, she guessed because he seemed focused on her lips. "You want a copy of the details of the will?"

"No." Rhia was quite sure about them since they'd poured over those details already. "When we looked at them, did you take note, for example, of exactly when you were made the beneficiary?"

"She made the will about a year before she died but had stipulated I shouldn't be informed of it till after she was buried."

"Mmm…" Rhia was puzzled. It was still quite a touchy subject for Luke, but she couldn't help thinking it was a bit late to make your will when you were around ninety. Then again maybe a previous will had indicated something like a charity…or the state.

She made it a point to investigate why there was that very odd bit about leaving the place to rot.

"I'm going to go the local church tomorrow to look at their records, though I don't imagine they'll go back as far as the earliest inhabitants of Greywood Hall," she told him.

"Sounds like a good plan."

"Then, after the church, I'll go on to the local library to see what I can find out there about the Greywood family. It might give me good insight into some of the forebears more quickly than pouring over the library records here at Greywood."

"Sounds good, too."

"I haven't told you yet, but the huge family bible in the library has given me a lot of names to start with since the family recorded births and deaths on it."

"Am I on it?" Amusement sparkled though she knew he was kidding.

"Sorry. I'm afraid not. Not your mother Elizabeth either. Elizabeth's not a handed down Greywood family name."

"We need to stay here at the cottage for a bit longer than I first imagined Rhia," Luke informed her when she got home from Greywood the next evening. "The whole house is going to be rewired during the next few days to match up to current specification, and it will be pretty messy."

"Okay. I'll make sure I check in with Mike about where to avoid. He's a nice guy."

"Nice guy?" He stopped her from heading to the kitchen. "Nicer than me?

"Not going there, Luke!"

It was quite unexpected when his hands snaked around her waist. The kiss which followed lingered.

"It's been quiet around here this afternoon."

Rhia's disbelieving laugh pealed out. "I don't believe that for a minute. That phone buzzes constantly."

"Well, maybe I just missed you."

A pause followed. Rhia wasn't sure what to make of his words, or his gaze.

"I saw some plumbing materials being delivered today," she ventured swallowing the moment. "Are the new bathrooms going in soon as well?"

"Not quite that soon." Luke laughed at her eager tone. "I got the planning permission today for the creation of the new rooms needed for en-suite bathrooms and the permits for the plasterwork requirements, but they'll take a little longer to create." His tone became a teasing chuckle. "As you once told me, the architectural changes need to be done sensitively."

Rhia remembered how she'd almost challenged his integrity.

"I'm sorry about that," she grinned. "I was pissed at you that day. Okay! Now you've had my bit of grovelling."

"I knew you were." He went back to serious mode. "I want you to attend my first meeting tomorrow morning with my interior decorator." His arms locked around her, trapping her at the sink.

"Why? I'm not an interior decorator. What do you expect from me?"

Rhia was delighted when he told her he was entirely happy with the services his decorator had provided before but emphasised that almost all of the previous facilities had been created for corporate use.

"I want you there to ensure that the decorative touches they might suggest are going to be correct for a private family home."

"What makes you think I can do that?"

"This little cottage has a homely feel about it, Rhia. Your personal touches are everywhere I look."

She was amazingly pleased with his answer. They discussed what sort of decorative style he imagined Greywood should have, Rhia clearly glad that he wanted some of the rooms to retain the grandeur that Greywood should display, yet still be a home people could happily live in with modern comforts and contemporary accessories where appropriate.

In turn, she was pleased to update him with her work at the church and the library. "I think I've now got sufficient to put together a reasonable family tree from the first Alexander Greywood who built the house in the late sixteen hundreds. His grave stone is still there in the church yard, although the detail is difficult to read. There's a sectioned off area of the graveyard for the Greywood family, including the more expected mausoleum building for the Victorian era."

The meeting the following morning was a revelation to Rhia. It shouldn't have been because she knew what a dynamic person Luke was, but the energy and verve he instilled in his employees was almost a measurable thing. His teams of workers enjoyed what they did and were energized by his work ethic.

It was exciting being part of the initial decorative planning, and she was happy to make her own observations where relevant. Luke's interior designer wasn't averse to having ideas put forward, was in fact quite used to Luke's input and suggestions so any comments she herself made were considered.

After leaving the dining room where the meeting had been held, Luke dragged Rhia into the large room next to the library. She hadn't been in that part of the house for a couple of days and was astonished to see it was already laid out as a fully functioning office.

"It's ready for me to move into now since all the electrical wiring is completed. Until I moved into your little bedroom, I never realised my normal *modus operandi* is to march around so much. It's tried my patience no end being unable to pace more than three steps in any direction."

"So your office is moving from today?" Rhia wasn't surprised or offended because she'd realised how caged in he'd been.

"Yes. Jeremy is arriving soon and he'll be using this desk here." He indicated the one nearest the door. "Mine is that one over there. I'll be bringing over my personal belongings right away. Your spare room will be restored to an empty room again by tomorrow, and the office furniture that's currently in there will be moved into a smaller room on the ground floor here at Greywood as an office for Mike."

"You don't hang around much do you?"

Rhia was puzzled later that evening when Luke insisted that they dine out at the end of a very long and tiring day. She appreciated it no doubt fitted his normal lifestyle, but it didn't fit hers. "I don't need to be wined and dined every night," she insisted, sparking off one of their mild arguments.

"I want to sample everything that the area has to offer." His answer was urbane – so they ate out.

"Ready for my latest update?" she asked as their main courses were delivered. They'd segued into the habit of her giving him any major historical updates at dinner.

"Fire away."

"Okay, you should get your handkerchief ready. It's all a bit sad."

Luke's answer was wry as he tackled his food, "Isn't history peppered with sad happenings?"

"You're right." Rhia nodded. "So far, you know there have been Alexander Greywoods at Greywood Hall for centuries, as some of the portraits bear out."

Luke nodded, his attention focused.

"Well, to cut to the chase. I've found out that your Amelia Greywood was the granddaughter of Alexander Greywood the umpteenth."

Luke grinned at her expression. "The umpteenth? Is this a new erudite historical term?"

"I'll get you for that later, Salieri," Rhia threatened, waving her fork at him. "Listen up, boy!" Her mock tutor voice went unchallenged as Luke tucked into his succulent steak.

"I've not quite authenticated exactly how many Alexanders there have been because a few infant mortalities cloud the process."

She cut a bit of fish and put it into her mouth. "Anyway, Amelia's great-grandfather continued to make money around 1840 from the Greywood Thread Mill that was started in 1804 – a good time for manufacturers since they were producing clothing for the navy, and for the regiments."

She stopped for a breath and to pop a piece of artichoke into her mouth. "Following me?"

Luke answered around a mouthful of salad. "1805 The Battle of Trafalgar?"

"Wow! You're good." She grinned at him. "For an Aussie, I'm impressed."

"Have you forgotten that I was educated at top-notch English schools."

"Sure." Rhia shrugged as she tackled more of her mouth-watering fish. "That fact slipped my mind for a moment."

"Continue, please."

"Okay. They also had a string of Greywood Drapers' shops here in northern England, which for a while brought in a tidy profit. Till Amelia's own dear grand-daddy – also an Alexander, born 1852 – seemed to put the scuppers on that. As far as I can tell, he was a wastrel and worked his way through quite a fortune. Most of the shops were sold and the mill closed down by 1889, though I've yet to scrutinize the estate records which should authenticate that."

"So you're thinking that by the time Amelia came along, the funds were already drying up?"

"Most certainly, but it's far more complicated than that. Her grandfather Alexander had three daughters but no surviving sons, which in the way of things probably pissed him off rather a lot. You know there was that snobby inheritance thing?"

Luke nodded.

"Well, there wasn't even a sickliest, weakling Alexander who struggled past infancy to maturity to get hands on the money!"

"Rhia Ashton! I'm shocked that as a historian you can be so glib." From Luke's wide smile and twinkling green eyes she knew exactly how serious he was.

She ignored the slight on her professionalism and finished off her main course before continuing. "The eldest of these three daughters, Lucinda, married in 1902 and went to live in Cornwall. According to one diary I've dipped into, she rarely returned to Greywood Hall."

Luke signalled the waiter to top up their wine glasses when their dessert was delivered.

"The middle daughter, Jocasta, born 1888, lived at Greywood till she was approximately twenty-two. The trail for her mysteriously stops around 1910."

"The Jo-Jo of the broken leg?"

Rhia chortled around her sorbet. "The very one!"

"So her broken limb didn't kill her?"

"No. But there remains some mystery about what happened to her around 1910."

"And the youngest of the three?"

"I've found evidence that Bethany, born 1892, eventually inherited Greywood in 1920 – long after her father died in February, 1911."

"Bethany, as the youngest, inherited?"

Rhia slipped cool mango sorbet between her lips. Luke followed as names and dates tripped off her tongue but she could see he also wanted to sample her delicious dessert. Without stopping her conversation, she held out a forkful for sampling.

"Mmm…delicious," he replied.

"Want to hear the rest?"

The simple nod had her continuing.

Rhia found she was enjoying the man's company far too much. "Well. Bethany was the youngest, but the estate eventually worked its way to her by 1920."

"Sounds like this is where the handkerchief is needed?"

"Yep." Rhia's enthusiasm overflowed. "The process of Bethany's inheritance was really slow because the eldest, Lucinda – as first daughter – became heir when their father Alexander died. Unfortunately, Lucinda also died two weeks later in March 1911 during the confinement of a stillborn daughter. According to one of the diaries, the poor woman only had one surviving poorly daughter named Melanie who was born in 1904. Lucinda had had a string of miscarriages over the years and was never in great health. Lucinda's daughter Melanie then became the official heir."

Luke complimented her on her sleuthing but needed something clarified. "Wouldn't the estate have passed on to some distant male heir when Alexander the howevermuch died?"

Rhia's burst of laughter startled the diners at the nearest table, causing her to make her apologies. "I love the howevermuch! I must use that one again," she chuckled before resuming. "The answer is no, because as far as I can tell there was no problem about a female being the heir. Victorian Society was riddled with new fangled ideas and lots of innovative practices, so I'm guessing Alexander wanted to keep the estate for his own children and changed his will accordingly."

"Or maybe because it isn't such a large estate in the scheme of English estates?" Luke was speculating too.

"Probably." Rhia agreed because there were no upper-echelon aristocratic rules in place. "Remember, their money came from trade, so the purely male heir thing would probably have just been snobbery. Trade families never quite had the same hang-ups about women inheriting. The problem was sometimes about unmarried women being able to spend their inherited wealth."

"Poor fragile women, unable to manage their finances, always needed the firm hand of a strong man to help them survive and keep them happy, and fulfilled." Luke grinned at her, the green of his eyes darkening. "Just like you, Rhia?"

"Don't go there if you value something you hold dear below your belt, Luke Salieri."

She tactfully resumed her tale. "After the deaths of both Alexander and Lucinda, the estate officially belonged to the ailing seven-year-old Melanie. Bethany's diary indicates that because of the health of the child her father, John Trevanyan, never brought her from Cornwall to visit Greywood Hall. As Melanie's executor Trevanyan was quite happy for Bethany to remain at Greywood and continue to run the place. Any disposable money, whatever was left after her father's profligate lifestyle had decimated it, remained in the hands of Trevanyan after the death of Melanie in December 1912."

"Okay. So Melanie had inherited it after her mother died."

Rhia nodded.

Luke continued, "The estate and some money that was left from Alexander?"

"Yes." Rhia finished her dessert and laid down the cutlery. "Bethany's diary indicates that Alexander left £10,000 pounds to Jocasta, and £10,000 to herself. The rest all went to Lucinda, and thus to Melanie, but I haven't found the exact amount of money yet."

"I'm guessing that was still quite a tidy sum for Jocasta in 1911?" Luke asked.

"Sure, if you considered it as your sort of pin money…but that wasn't nearly enough for Bethany to run the estate as you'll hear, if you let me finish this sorry tale."

She sipped the last of her wine while her coffee was poured. "This is where it gets complicated. Melanie was, of course, a minor. Her father, as her next of kin, was deemed to be the recipient of anything that belonged to her."

"Was that usual?"

"I think it wasn't too unheard of."

Luke sipped his coffee. "So why did Bethany inherit? If it went to Trevanyan after his daughter's death?"

"I've no official documentation to back this up yet, but from Bethany's diary and the internet searches I've done, John Trevanyan was fairly well set up himself and already had a sizeable estate in Cornwall. He didn't want anything at all to do with Greywood Hall. Bethany's diary states that Trevanyan officially got the ownership of Greywood transferred back to Jocasta about two months after Melanie died."

"But he kept any cash that Lucinda, then Melanie inherited?"

"It seems so."

Luke rubbed his chin fingering the light stubble. "So you're saying that the estate became Jocasta's, but with no money to run it?"

"Yes. Except she was missing. From well before her father died. She went off on a visit with friends, to Naples, in July 1910 and never returned to Greywood Hall."

"Never?" Luke's ears perked up at that one. "What about the friends? Didn't any of them know where she was?"

"No. It appears they parted company when Jocasta went on to Florence and they returned home. Her trail ends at that point. Again, this is from what I can track from other sources, and according to the diaries, but as you know I've only dipped a toe in the water regarding them."

"So, Greywood Hall and £10,000 belongs to Jocasta but she doesn't know about any of these deaths? Or about her portion?"

"I've no reason, or evidence yet, to believe she knew," Rhia clarified as they left the restaurant. They climbed into a taxi because Luke preferred not to drive when they ate out locally.

They continued the conversation in the back of the vehicle, comfortably close. "Bethany is quite distraught at times in the diary. It's painful to read some of the heart-rending entries that detail the lengths she and her lawyer went to, to locate her sister. They even paid a private detective, a retired police officer, to find Jocasta but it seems he drew a blank too, and Bethany's resources weren't sufficient for her to continue."

"Well, you've certainly uncovered much more about the Greywood family than I would have been able to at this stage." He paid off the taxi on their arrival back to the cottage. "That's it so far?"

"Nearly. Due to Jocasta's continued absence Bethany and her lawyer eventually had to assume something dire had happened to her sister. It took the stipulated period after that to officially declare Jocasta dead. By then it was 1920."

In the sitting room she nestled next to Luke on the couch. "The youngest one, Bethany, lived at Greywood all her life. She never married but her diaries divulge that she had a sweetheart during the First World War. Unfortunately he died without knowing he had made Bethany pregnant during one of his home visits."

"He was a local man?"

"Fairly local. He was from Skipton. He'd been shipped home to recuperate in late 1917. He spent six months recovering from a bayonet that pierced his lung, and of course the mustard gas he'd breathed in had done damage as well."

"Guess his recovery was sufficient if he got Bethany pregnant?" Luke's eyes were twinkling as he took her hand in a light grasp.

"You guess right. Unfortunately, he was sent back to France in April 1918, and his tragic death just one month later devastated Bethany. She gave birth to an illegitimate daughter, Amelia, in early December 1918 who was brought up here at Greywood, although to do so was a scandal at the time. Unmarried ladies palmed their illegitimate children off to an orphanage, or to families who'd rear the child."

Luke's arm snaked comfortably across her shoulder.

"Of course by then Bethany had no elder relatives to dictate to her and I suppose at that time she had just sufficient monetary resources to fly in the face of convention. In the fullness of time Bethany died leaving the property to Amelia."

"And I'm guessing, since her name was still Greywood, Amelia never married?"

"Correct, although she seems to have carved a niche for herself in local society even though she was illegitimate. I'm finding a lot to respect about Amelia Greywood," Rhia answered vehemently. "The sources of income dried up, and she had to make huge economies during her life, selling many of Greywood's treasures just to keep the wolf from the door."

But none of that explained why Luke was the one on the dotted line of her will.

Chapter Ten

"This place is magic, Luke," Rhia enthused after a beautifully presented meal on the Saturday night.

The ambience was extremely romantic, Luke unaware of just how ideal the setting was when he'd booked. The subdued lighting, tastefully low music from the live band, plus the excellent décor, added to the dreamy character and didn't help his crusade to disengage himself from her allure.

He wanted to do more than give her a chaste goodnight kiss.

"I heard of this place but never had an opportunity to come."

Rhia clutched his hand across the table and squeezed her appreciation, her fingers lingering to entwine themselves around his, a bit like her whole presence was welding itself around him. "Thanks for insisting we come. I wouldn't have wanted to miss this place."

By the time their coffee and liqueurs arrived, their conversation was strumming with an extra tension.

"I'll just pop into the ladies before we head home," Rhia whispered.

She rejoined him at the taxi he'd ordered just as he finished a call. It rang again. He cursed in Italian, reluctant to answer. Switching his mobile off during their meal was a habit he'd adopted, but he was now fuming as he slapped it off again and pocketed it before opening the taxi door for her.

"I need to make another flying visit to London tomorrow."

He was so livid that he didn't risk speaking any more to Rhia in case he bit her nose off. She definitely didn't deserve any of his ire.

His anger had dissipated though by the time they reached her cottage.

***

After lying in bed longer than usual, Rhia sloped her way into the shower to make a start on the day, resigned to not seeing Luke till much later. The pulsating throb of a landline telephone accompanied her tuneless singing: not the one downstairs in her hall, for the sound was too close by for that. It had to be the extension that had been put in for Luke's temporary office and was the only reminder left in the room. She let it ring knowing that any business automatically transferred to the new number at Greywood Hall.

The fine summer weather seemed to have eventually broken, rain sheeting her bedroom window as she towelled herself dry. Warmer clothes were needed as she rifled amongst her wardrobe contents for a pair of jeans and a jumper. Brushing her hair into shape, the insistent ringing of the same telephone became very annoying. For the first time she invaded the privacy of Luke's former provisional office to pick up the receiver.

"Luke!"

The strident word blasted Rhia's ear off. "I'm sorry, Luke's not here just now."

"I want to speak to Luke."

"Luke's not here just now," she repeated. "May I take a message for him?"

"Why are you answering the phone instead of Jeremy? Pass me on to Luke, now!"

Rhia decided after only a few more words that she'd had enough of this extremely rude woman. "As I said already, Luke isn't available. Please tell me what I can do for you?"

"I'll get Luke to fire you, you moron!"

Moron? Rhia's blood boiled but she didn't want to cause any offence to a customer, or even a colleague of Luke's, so she forced herself to remain calm. "If you give me your name," she tried one last and final time, "I'll tell Luke you called."

The words that followed shocked Rhia to the core.

"Fine. Just tell him that his girlfriend Danielle called and that I won't make it for our dinner date this evening. He can come to my flat instead. I'll be home by ten thirty."

Girlfriend? Who was this woman?

Silence descended leaving Rhia with a dead phone and an even deader lump where her heart should have been.

Why was Luke meeting this Danielle person for dinner? And why, more importantly, did this Danielle assume it would be easy for Luke to go to her flat at ten thirty? Rhia's stomach plunged to the carpet. Had Luke met up with this female the night he'd spent in London, last Saturday, and had he gone back to her today? More importantly, what had he been doing with the horrible woman?

"Bloody bitch!" She didn't quite know who she was most angry with, but she certainly wasn't happy with Luke.

Later that afternoon he phoned.

"Hello, Rhia."

He had no idea how much his cheery greeting affected her. She'd had all day though to prepare herself for his call.

"You had a call this morning on the cottage temporary office phone," she informed him.

"I thought all calls were transferring to Greywood?" His answer was blithe, unaware.

"Your girlfriend – Danielle I believe her name is – says to tell you she'll not make your dinner date tonight, but you can pop round to her flat after ten-thirty. It seems she'll be home by then," Rhia managed to inform him tonelessly.

The silence at the other end spoke volumes before she heard what she imagined was a tirade of creative Italian cursing. "It's not how it seems, Rhia."

"I don't want to know, Luke, how it seems, but if you're already reneging on our signed agreement you can cancel our wedding. I refuse to share a husband with anyone, especially not with a bitch like Danielle." Rhia zapped off her phone.

Luke didn't try to contact her again but returned that night around nine-thirty, no overnight stay involved, but too late for dinner. She had given up on him anyway and had picked at her own food earlier, chucking most of it in the bin.

Their wedding was supposed to be the next day.

"Rhia!" His bellow would have wakened a great white bear in the North Pole as he thundered upstairs.

She was upstairs in bed, a book in her hands, when Luke erupted into her room. Striding close to the bed he ignored her body language that screamed at him to keep the hell away.

"Rhia, you have to believe me."

Luke was spitting angry but he couldn't possibly be as angry as she was. She ignored him. He waited. She ignored him even more. Exasperated he stomped away from the bed.

Th word uproar was a pretty good description of his volume. "I am not having an affair with Danielle."

More of the same followed, some of it English and some Italian, but try as he might Rhia refused to look at him, every thing about her furious as she pretended to read.

"We are getting married tomorrow, Rhia," he persisted, lowering to a minor roar. "There's no damned way you're welching out on our deal. You said you'd marry me and you will."

His jacket was ripped off and flung askew. Her ears rang like a clarion but she refused to acknowledge it as he ranted on.

"You've signed that bloody contract and Greywood needs you now. What you've started you have to finish."

Bloody Hell! The way she was feeling she'd easily leave him high and dry …but Greywood?

She eventually lifted her head. Luke's natural olive skin tone was leached to a greyish white. Too bad. He deserved to feel as sick as she'd been feeling all day. Her words were a whisper. "Who is Danielle?"

"Nobody important," he answered into the dark and sinister cloud that enveloped them. His rage was under wraps now, subdued by her example. At her unimpressed glare he added, "She's a woman I was dating before I met you."

Rhia exhaled, her chest heaving with the effort of replying. "Before you met me or…" her voice trembled on the last word "…still?"

"Still?"

"Last weekend in London?" Her eyes were the sharpest darts, very pained darts, but she didn't really care now if Luke noticed, or not. "Did you meet up with her then?" Her chin wobbled on the last, so difficult had it been to get the words out, but there was no way she was going to be palmed off with lies or platitudes.

"Sod it! I'm not going to lie to you."

Luke wrenched off his tie to the beat of more impressive Italian swearing. Plonking himself down on the edge of the bed beside her, he took a deep breath before cautiously replying.

"Yes, I saw her in London last weekend."

Rhia moved away from him.

"Danielle came, uninvited, to my office. But it was daytime." His hands slid forward to cover hers where she held the edges of the book.

"Daytime? What has daytime got to do with it Luke? What does the time of day matter?"

"I told Danielle ages ago that the relationship I'd had with her was long finished. And I told her last week, too, when she turned up like a bad penny."

Rhia scoffed. A single tear slid down her cheek as she wrenched her hands free. "But she doesn't believe that, does she, if she called again today?"

"She may not have this morning, but she damned well understands now." His temper was again only just under control as he ploughed his fingers through his dishevelled mop.

"Do you really think she's someone who listens very well?" Rhia's mockery bit deep as she swiped another tear away.

"She knows we're getting married tomorrow, so the message should eventually get through her avaricious head."

One long finger dared to reach forward catching the drip on her chin. She whipped his finger away as quick as a fly swat.

"How can I trust that she won't be replaced by someone similar when you're away from home, Luke?" She wasn't so naïve that she didn't acknowledge just how attractive he was to women.

Luke had a good solution.

"We won't ever separate. If I need to be in London, you'll come with me, even if it's only for one night. I know you don't want to listen to me right now, but I honestly will be faithful to you. I will honour my contract with you."

He needed to be sure she'd honour the agreement made for their year. For Greywood. She knew that.

"You'd better not be lying to me, Luke Salieri. Not now and not ever."

"I don't tell lies, Rhia."

She'd never seen pain in Luke's eyes before, but she was seeing it now.

Grudgingly she accepted the olive branch for what it was. "I really hate myself for saying this just now, but I will marry you tomorrow."

"Thank you. Let me explain about Danielle."

"No. You don't need to tell me anything."

"I do. You know I do, otherwise it'll be a festering wound that will magnify at the worst possible time. I want to have no secrets between us."

"No secrets." Her voice wobbled again.

Luke took her hand and exhaled loudly. She felt the tension drain out of him as it drained out of her.

"Danielle is someone I dated on five occasions. The last time I saw her was three weeks before I went on my last trip to Australia, which was five weeks before I met you. I told her then that we'd not be seeing each other again. Unfortunately, as you realised, she doesn't take rejection well. She liked the idea of milking my money, loved being seen at the most popular high class venues. She pestered me on my cell and kept ringing the London office even after I went to Australia. I instructed Jeremy, more than once, to never pass on her calls to me."

Rhia recalled hearing those very words instructed herself.

"While Jeremy was up here on one of his quick visits someone else in the London office gave her the cottage number and she called here numerous times after I set up office here."

"Persistent bitch!"

"Yes, she is that. She tried my cell again last night, just before we came home, telling me she'd made a restaurant booking for this evening and expected me to be there. I realised I'd have to see her face to face to tell her to back off, so I arranged the impromptu visit to London."

"Were you at any business meetings at all today?" Rhia had to know.

"Yes, one that had been scheduled even before I went to Australia, but an appointment I'd cancelled when I knew I needed to spend more time at Greywood. I rescheduled it before lunch today, and then I met Danielle at one o'clock in the little bistro near my office. I bought two coffees, not even any hint of food which she ranted about, then I spent a matter of minutes telling her in no uncertain terms that I was not ever going out with her again and that she was verging on entering the realms of being a stalker."

"What made her think you'd see her tonight? Is she the most stupid woman in the world, or what?" Rhia was incensed on his behalf.

"Her parting words at the bistro were that she would go to the press and give them details of our affair if I didn't relent."

"She's a delusional idiot." Rhia sat forward. "Tell me you socked her in the jaw."

"Violence woman, will get you nowhere," Luke chuckled. "I had nothing to hide and I won't bow down to anyone's blackmail."

They looked at each other and flew into a fit of giggles remembering their own bizarre arrangement – what Amelia Greywood had done to them was a definite form of blackmail.

When they'd stopped laughing Rhia managed to add, "But what will you do if she goes to the press?"

"What's she going to say? That we went out a few times? I never wrote any love poems or sent her lewd phone pictures. She'll have no record of anything remotely damaging on her voice mail – all I ever remember saying was where we'd meet and when."

"So what on earth does she think she has on you that would be newsworthy?"

Luke shrugged saying he'd no idea. "Beats me! There was only sex involved between us once, not even on every date, and I'm not proud to admit I felt lust only that one time because…" His hands raked through his thick hair, his eyes self-mocking. "She was all over me like a rash, I guess. Suffice to say sex happened and then afterwards I went home."

"Don't you think she might have a little something else, if she's trying to bribe you like this?"

"No. Unless it's because she wants to damage my self-esteem. She might say that I can't perform in the sack…or, that my equipment is sub-standard?"

Rhia gaped. "If the bitch does that I'll send in a statement categorically refuting it. But I'd do it in such a way that would annihilate her."

"That would be very commendable, Rhia, but I'd not want you to perjure yourself."

A long look passed between them, and lasted till she gave him a gentle push.

"Go to your own bed, Luke. I've heard enough."

He took the hint.

Rhia was up before Luke the next morning. When she passed by, his bedroom door was wide open. He lay fast asleep, the bedcovers barely covering him, an indication that he probably had had a restless night.

Looking at his face in repose, she knew she could easily come to love him. She'd signed herself up for this marriage initially under a degree of coercion, but now it was unbearable to think of him with anyone else. She was definitely going to marry him that afternoon, and she was going to make sure he never ever had cause to stray, but she wasn't going to let him think she was a push-over either. Temptation had faced her the previous evening but she'd managed to resist: not because she was prudish; but more because she didn't trust her own emotions.

She quickly showered and dressed. Unable to face speaking to him yet she took the coward's way out. A note was left beside the coffee that she'd prepared saying she was out walking Thor before going along to Greywood Hall.

***

Luke felt like shit when he came to, having tossed and turned all night, his mind continually chewing over the situation. Rhia was only supposed to be a temporary feature for a year of his life, after which they'd say goodbye and go their own ways. It bothered him that it seemed to matter so much that she was happy with the strange arrangement. Dawn had been almost breaking

137

when he eventually nodded off, still with no answers to his own questions.

Dribbling himself downstairs, he read her little sticky note and saw it for the cop-out it really was. Grabbing a juice and coffee, he got himself ready for what was going to be a momentous day.

A short while later he tracked her down in the library. He couldn't start on any of his work till he'd at least seen her and knew how she was feeling. She must go ahead with the marriage later that afternoon without question – he wouldn't allow or contemplate any other result than that.

He needed her.

"What do you have planned for today?" he asked.

Her tone was cool; dispassionate. That was a first since she was always bubbling full of optimism about her work. It took seconds to realise she was avoiding eye contact again, and she'd returned to the stand-back-from-me-buddy body language.

"I'm amassing all the paperwork I found upstairs and intend to store it all in here for later investigation. Trips up and down will take the best part of the day I should imagine."

Their meeting was brief and not at all private since members of Luke's usual team who took inventory were in the library with Rhia.

"If we head back to the cottage about four p.m. is that time enough for you?"

Luke's question was delicately phrased since he had absolutely no idea if Rhia was going to change clothes for their wedding at five o'clock. He had no idea if, in her present frame of mind, she'd stand beside him and take her vows wearing the jeans she was currently dressed in. Shocked at himself, he found he didn't care a hoot what she wore, so long as she was there and said the right words and signed the damned bit of paper. No way was she copping out of it. He would put the pen in her hand if need be, but she would marry him.

"I'll make my own way over and see you just before five at the cottage." Her tone continued, unforgiving.

That gave him a slight dilemma. The suit he planned to wear was hanging in the spare room wardrobe so he needed access to the house for the time it would take him to shower, shave and dress. There was absolutely no way he wasn't going through with those procedures, even though he acknowledged their unorthodox circumstances.

At twenty to five, Luke arrived at the cottage. Hearing Rhia talk to Thor in the garden meant he was able to nip upstairs and sort himself out. Back down in record time he greeted the registrar just before Jeremy and Roger arrived, cutting it fine at a few minutes before five o'clock. Rhia had prepared her back garden table for the necessary signing of the documents; a simple vase of flowers freshly picked from the flowerbeds decorating the wooden surface.

An unsmiling Rhia joined them, absolutely stunning in a long white gown, Thor padding at her side as her only attendant. He was unable to take his eyes off the vision she made. Not quite the fairy sprite of the woods that he had originally imagined but a sexy goddess, draped in body hugging silk.

Just before the ceremony started, he was startled when Roger asked the registrar to pause for a few seconds. Roger dashed down the garden to hastily break off flowering blooms and some matching foliage. Having deftly wrapped some long grasses around the stems Roger then presented it as a simple spray to Rhia.

"Every beautiful bride should have a bouquet." Roger's statement was formal. "And there's no doubt you deserve these, Miss Ashton."

He noticed that Roger's kind statement had made her eyes glisten.

She would only be Miss Ashton for a few seconds more. She would have his name in mere moments. A tiny sweat trickled down his back. Nothing could stop her being his wife now.

As well as the hint of fear, a good dose of chagrin oozed down there as well and he couldn't for the life of him work out why that should be so.

Though he'd originally given some consideration to what Rhia would wear in his fantasies – and to what he was currently wearing for the ceremony – he hadn't thought about all the other traditional wedding trappings. Bouquets. Cake. Venue. People. Photographs.

Roger's simple gesture tweaked his conscience, but thrusting it aside he consoled himself that their wedding wasn't supposed to be a normal one.

They said their vows.

The word love was a tiny part of the standard ceremony given by the registrar since they hadn't opted to write their own. He parroted the words after the celebrant, as did Rhia.

He clasped her hands when they were instructed to kiss at the end of the ceremony. Unwilling for her to pull back from him at such an eventful moment, he made sure the kiss was thorough. Though stiff in his grasp, she complied.

Jeremy and Roger signed the certificate after them, and it was all over in minutes.

After a celebratory sip of champagne, the registrar departed.

Then, when the taxi arrived for the four of them, they went to a nearby restaurant for a quiet but convivial early evening meal – simple – no frills and definitely no wedding cake.

If the circumstances of the marriage seemed very unusual, neither of his employees was crass enough to make it evident. The talk was kept to the general, but, although she joined in, Rhia wasn't nearly as exuberant as he knew her to be at other times.

After the meal, he ushered her into a taxi, the other two heading off to the hotel booked for them.

Conversation in their taxi was artificial and no matter how hard he tried he couldn't seem to make it any different.

Thor barked like mad in the back enclosure on their arrival.

"I know he needs out, Rhia, but please, not just yet." His words were a begged whisper. "You look absolutely beautiful and I want to thank you for what you've just done."

"I did it for Greywood."

"I know you did, but I want to reassure you about everything you've signed up for. The way you look right now, I want to rush you straight upstairs and rip off that gorgeous gown. Then I'd love to make love to you until you beg me to stop. But I won't."

"You won't?"

"No." He searched her eyes to gauge her mood since she'd been so solemn. "For the rest of the year, we can share the house and cohabit just as we have done for the last few days, if that's your preference. If you want me to move into your room and make love as man and wife, then you'll call those shots. Either way, I will stick to my monogamy agreement. And there will be no other woman during the coming year."

"I appreciate your being candid, Luke. I've accepted your terms and I've signed your bit of paper. I'm now legally your wife and will honour all that will entail but, right now, I am going to take off my lovely dress." She raised her open palm on seeing a sparkle darken his eyes. A hint of a smile broke the tension that had been at her cheeks for the last few hours. "I can't possibly walk Thor in this. As for making love to you, if it happens it will be because we both really want it to and nothing to do with a bit of paper."

Chapter Eleven

"Tomorrow's the day, Rhia!"

Luke's excited whirling of her around and around sent the blood rushing to her head, spinning her so fast she could hardly breathe.

"What are you talking about?"

"I can't wait for us to move into Greywood Hall." Luke's enthusiastic verve was almost palpable. "The rooms we need are all ready now – nothing to keep us waiting."

Rhia beamed at him as he released her to the floor and hugged her tight. "You mean the still to be ready twenty or so rooms don't matter?"

"Nope!" Luke stole a kiss, something he'd lately been doing all the time. "In the grand scheme of Greywood Hall they'll get done, but we have everything we need for now, Mrs. Salieri."

Rhia's eyes widened, refraining from saying anything about his comment. He'd never called her that in a playful tone, never really called her that at all since he always made sure to introduce her to new people as my wife Rhia, but not Mrs. Salieri.

"So are you telling me in your devious way, Mr. Salieri, that you hate sleeping in my cottage?" She pretended to be in a huff.

"How could I when I have you to hold every single night."

It was true.

They hadn't slept apart for one single night since their marriage, Rhia having surprised him that night by inviting him into her room, telling him she was ready to sample what he had to offer.

They'd been married for five weeks, and although Luke had expected to have moved into Greywood sooner, he'd had to prioritise his man-resources at two of his other work sites, slowing down the progress at Greywood. Business was business, and when all was said and done, it really didn't matter all that much since they only slept at the cottage. Their days were occupied at Greywood, and with continual updates to the local lawyer, they still fulfilled the will conditions when Luke made a few business trips away from home, Rhia accompanying him.

"How can we celebrate our moving into Greywood?" he asked.

He was in his favourite place, holding her with her body welded to his own, his arms draped across her shoulders.

"It's too soon for a champagne reception. The main rooms aren't all ready."

His question was almost forgotten as he kissed her, but her eventual reply seemed to please him.

"How about we wait till the restoration is totally complete and then we'll invite everybody for a spectacularly different kind of party." Struggling out of his tempting arms, she twirled in circles, arms akimbo. "A restoration event sounds just right to me, where we're all dressed in period costume and…"

"Excellent idea! But for now we'll have an early sampling of the cases of champagne that were delivered today."

Rhia organised the removal of their clothes and personal belongings from the cottage to Greywood the following day but left everything else.

The main kitchen at Greywood had been fabulously upgraded. All the historic utensils were either displayed somewhere where possible, or stored carefully in the attics till further notice when decisions would be made about where they should go. She'd agreed with the designer that although she valued them as artefacts, she didn't actually want to cook with them – modern appliances were too well loved. The kitchen décor was extremely suitable for a grand old house, but it was stuffed with state of the art equipment.

Eating out every night wasn't necessary. More often she got her own way, and either she cooked for Luke, or together they rustled up something to eat, though he was still very much the novice in the kitchen.

Greywood Hall was proving to be such a fun house to live in.

After dinner one evening Rhia divulged her latest bit of news.

"I can't make head or tail of it, Luke." She flashed a small piece of faded white lined paper and an even more fragile piece of blue airmail paper at him. "Amelia wasn't inclined to go gallivanting, as far as I have found out at this point. Not enough money for anything like that most of the time."

He had already learned to let her emotions vent if she was in her 'terrier mode'. "But surely even poor Amelia was due the occasional holiday?"

Rhia's research had uncovered that Amelia had gone to university, gaining an English Literature degree, but she'd only ever worked part time with a local children's charity. This had earned her lots of kudos but little money. Very much required money.

"Of course she was." Rhia paced around their den – one of his favourite rooms. "But this trip was in the late 1970s. Back then, any trip to Australia was incredibly expensive. Air fares were astronomical. People saved up for years to pay for them."

"Yet you've already found out she managed the occasional trips to Europe."

"Well yes," she exhaled loudly in front of him. "And we know too well she sacrificed quite a few paintings for that, Luke."

"So what did she sell to finance the trip to Australia?" He was curious now.

"Her bank account was credited with money from the sale of some Victorian jewellery."

His eyebrows rose appropriately at her sleuthing.

"I found receipts for considerable sums for a diamond necklace and a Victorian pearl choker."

That information didn't particularly bother him, but Rhia's agitation did so he tried to trap her. "But why is this particular trip annoying you so much?"

"She financed the trip by selling off valuable jewellery, probably the last of her collection, for a trip that lasted only four days."

He'd often journeyed back to Australia to sort out some business panic, trips that hadn't been much longer than four days. He told her about them but couldn't appreciate why she was still so uptight.

Slumping onto the couch, she clutched the pieces of paper like a lifeline. The white one she flashed again in front of his nose when he sat beside her.

"This is an itinerary, Luke. It details her flight from Heathrow to Brisbane with three stops at airports along the way. There are no hotels or cushy layovers as far as I can tell, just boring very long delays for refuelling and necessaries."

No way was he inclined to stop her tirade.

"She's noted the hotel she stayed at in Brisbane for three nights, and then she repeated the whole journey back to England."

Luke still couldn't see that as being a problem since he would probably do it himself if he needed to.

"All that expense for three nights in Australia? In the 1970s?"

He waited.

"Who would have gone to Australia at vast expense for only three days? As far as I can tell she saw virtually nothing of the country. She travelled for more time than she actually set foot on Australian soil."

"What's in the airmail letter?" He patiently indicated the blue paper.

"This?" Rhia's voice grew subdued as she held it aloft. "This is merely an acknowledgement from someone in Brisbane who confirms that it was very pleasant to meet her and thanks her for doing business with him. The postal date was just after her trip."

"That's it?"

"That's it." Rhia sank into gloom.

"Well, at least she had one trip to my place of birth," he chuckled. "That's surely the best connection to me yet?"

"Luke, the trip was made when you were two months old."

***

The next months at Greywood Hall continued to be a busy time for both of them. Rhia had thought that her routine would consist of daytime research and night times in Luke's arms but it turned out to be a little more varied than that.

Improvements made to Greywood Hall were pretty standard fare for Luke and his teams. By that time there were five other sites being currently remodelled in England, the squads of workmen Luke employed a well-oiled machine, rotating from site to site, coming to Greywood Hall when it was most suitable for their particular work schedules.

"I can't believe the other venues can remain unique." Her tone was sceptic, thinking that the renovated places would be clones of each other.

"We'll visit them all, you doubting Thomas, and then you can tell me just how distinctive we've made them." His winning smile said that he wasn't offended by her cynicism.

Rhia found that each venue had, indeed, retained its original character. She was fascinated by the expertise involved in getting the sites ready for corporate hire, but also seriously impressed by the speed at which it was all happening.

After visiting the other five sites she was fully cognisant of the fact that it only transpired because Luke delegated many decisions to his very competent management team, though the final decisions always rested with him.

Luke leased a small fleet of helicopters which whizzed between the venues, transporting personnel more efficiently than by road. Rhia felt she was climbing into one of them, or a chartered jet, as often as she stepped into her car. It wasn't exactly true but before Luke had catapulted into her life, she'd hardly ever flown in anything.

Greywood Hall had money piled into it where necessary, Luke seemingly a bottomless pit of the stuff. Solar heating systems and other devices to reduce the carbon footprint were put in place. Since the window frames all required replacing, special glass had been installed to improve heat loss in winter and address the need for rooms to be cooler in summer – all in keeping with the original style of the building.

"The stonemasons have done a superb job." Rhia's compliment came after the final outside work was completed. "The new curving forestairs are fabulously grand – just like they must have been when the house was originally built. And the terrace is perfect to walk on now."

They'd been entering Greywood from the back kitchen doorway for weeks while the front of the house was being worked on. The stone facade of the building was now blasted clean, the timber of the new window frames gleamed and the roof slates had been replaced. She wasn't joking; it really did look tremendous. "You asked me ages ago what we should do to celebrate moving into Greywood…"

Luke grabbed her and kissed her before she could even finish the sentence.

"Stop!" she protested. "I'm trying to have a serious conversation here."

"Okay. Spill quickly, and then I can make a serious attack on your gorgeous body." Luke released her long enough for her to continue.

"Right. I'm not butting in here, I hope, but if you want to make any kind of memorable event for the completion of the renovations why not host something like a Masked Ball, or a Period Dress event, like I mentioned a while ago?"

Luke nodded and his lips did that little twitching thing that meant he was considering the idea.

"Remind me of that when we get closer to the end of renovations," he declared, snuggling into her neck.

The front curves of steps were a magnificent way to ascend to the impressive hallway now sparklingly illuminated by the cleaned and renovated chandelier. Rhia was doubly impressed knowing that all the electric lighting was of the most effective and eco-friendly low energy adaptation. The interior decorating team, using local painters and decorators, had made fabulous inroads. All were changes Rhia was pleased to have been involved in, even if it was only a tiny bit.

The gardens were also looking impressive. She'd had a hand in those decisions too, at times disagreeing with Bob and June Renton, but they'd always come to some kind of compromise which pleased her no end.

It became a stately and grand house anyone would be proud to live in, yet despite all the new changes it retained a homely feel. Like Rhia's little cottage along the road, Greywood Hall now had lots of bright touches in fabrics, cushions and wall decorations and was filled with beautiful flower arrangements. At present the flowers were bought in, but the grand plan was that in the next few years a huge selection of flowers and vegetables could be harvested from the renovated and newly planted walled garden and re-glazed greenhouses.

Weeks passed by in a blur.

Rhia continued to discover amazing things about Amelia Greywood and the earlier occupants, but there was still nothing conclusive on why Luke had inherited. They'd given up trying to spend time together at lunchtime for interim updates, their work schedules not always convenient, but their other meals were always shared.

It was very domestic.

"London tomorrow," Luke informed her yet again. Around twice a week they flew to London when Luke went for meetings or business related social events.

"Okay," she answered around a mouthful of roast beef sandwich, "I'll ask Bob and June Renton to see to Thor. I'm so glad they love him just as much as we do."

On the occasions which did not offer Luke any leisure time, she popped in to the London museums while he saw to business matters.

When they were attending anything formal of an evening, she had acquiesced and had allowed Luke to add to her wardrobe so that she was decked in the most appropriate style for the occasion. It was easy to fall into the luxury lifestyle of living in supreme comfort in Luke's London apartment, but she didn't allow herself to think at all about how she'd miss it when the year was over. She felt she had acquitted herself well at the social events – the charity functions and business dinners they had attended. She was pretty sure Luke had been proud of her and people they met readily accepted her as his wife, not knowing anything about their situation.

***

"I'm really pissed off, Luke."

Rhia's mood was obviously not good. After more than six months living together Luke knew the best thing to do was let her blow, listen and then maybe make some suitable comment.

"You've had no update on my researches regarding your inheritance for ages. I purposely held back till I had something concrete, but all I've got is still a puddle of soft mush!"

Her disgusted tone left him in no doubt of just how frustrated and exasperated she was feeling. Settled into the comfortable couch in the modestly sized room they had decorated as a family den, he cradled his wine glass. Rhia strode around the room having set down hers on the nearest table when they'd retreated there after their dinner. He had sensed something was bothering her during their meal preparations but realised she wasn't ready to tell him at that point. They were both fairly good now at interpreting each other's moods.

After months of extensive research at Greywood Hall, Rhia had yet to make the final elusive connection between himself and his benefactress…and that lack of success really bugged her.

From his perspective, he now didn't really care what she'd uncover, although he still admitted to being curious about it. His initial drive to use Rhia's considerable skills for that task had dissipated. He loved that she was still so motivated to find out, but he hadn't found parting with his own money to restore Greywood Hall a chore. For the first time ever, he was beginning to feel he had a proper home, a place he was settling into comfortably like an old shoe – absolutely nothing like the cold and emotionless mansion his mother and father had inhabited and called home.

"Everything I've found leads to the assumption that your great-grandmother was Amelia Greywood's disappearing aunt Jocasta. It's the only thing that makes any sense, any sense at all."

Rhia had hinted at this a number of times before, but he'd rejected the possibility. She continued to pace about, dragging her hands through her hair, fanning it out from her ears, a cute habit he loved to watch.

"Are you sure your mother's name really was Elizabeth Low?"

"Definitely!" Luke was positive. "When my mother married my father she double-barrelled her name and called herself Elizabeth Low-Salieri. She always claimed it made good business sense. She deemed it was easier to keep at the helm of her father's engineering business when her name was almost the same as it had been pre-marriage."

"But you don't think that was why she did it?"

"I've told you already how much my mother revered her English origins. She really didn't want to take my father's name at all, but in those days it was unheard of for a married woman to retain her maiden name."

"Why wouldn't she have wanted your father's name?" Her question was cautious since she knew how prickly he was when discussing his mother.

"My mother was a snob. Probably the biggest snob in Brisbane." He laughed, but it was a hollow one. "In her estimation, Italian immigrants in Australia didn't quite have the same kudos, unlike anyone with a hint of upper echelon English backgrounds."

"Then, why on earth did she and your father get married?"

"I've never had a friggin' clue." He got up and also stomped around the room. "I never, in my twenty plus years with them, ever saw them kiss or hug each other. I don't even remember them ever laughing or smiling at each other. They didn't exactly hate each other, but they lived a sterile, extremely formal existence."

"And where did you fit in with that?"

Chapter Twelve

"Me? Fit in? You must be joking!" His derisory laugh was hollow to the point of pain. "I was trotted out occasionally to prove they had a son, but I can assure you, not that often. And rarely after I was sent to school in England at the age of seven."

"Luke, I'm so sorry they were mean to you."

Rhia stopped his pacing and hugged him tight aware that he itched to metaphorically free himself from the desperate loneliness of his youth.

His grip intensified, his lips hissing against her forehead. "They were never physically mean to me. It was just that for long periods of time I was out of sight, out of mind. Their separate business needs always came first for them. They employed the best nannies so they knew I was being well cared for."

"Materially looked after. It's not the same as love and care from your own parents."

"You've not exactly had it easy either." He remembered her telling him of her parents' divorce and the aftermath of it. "You're not exactly hunky dory with your father."

"My upbringing was a walk in the park compared to yours."

Rhia pulled his head down and kissed him thoroughly, kissed him with a passion that he felt right down to his toes.

"My mother loved me unconditionally till the day she died. In his own way, my father did what he could."

He cradled her gently as she continued.

"After my parents' separation my father did try his best to keep contact with me, even though he'd relocated to Belgium. He did love me and I always knew it. I was the one who couldn't handle his quick remarriage to a much younger Belgian woman. I was the one who rejected his second family."

"You felt he'd betrayed your mother?" Luke was trying to understand.

"A shrink would probably say yes. But really and truly?"

Luke watched the hurt and embarrassment fly across her features.

"I was just a spoiled little girl who didn't want to share. I couldn't handle him having other children that weren't my mother's."

"With our backgrounds," Luke growled into her ear, "neither of us has a clue about being a long term parent. That's why I never want to inflict the hurt and loneliness on offspring of mine. I never want children who could be tainted with the problems our parents have inflicted on us."

"Okay, I get that." Rhia's expression looked wounded when he drew back a little.

"Back to the Australian connection that isn't," she repeated. "Then if Elizabeth Low was definitely your mother's name, are you sure your maternal grandfather was called Alexander Low?"

"Again definitely."

He sat down on the couch, relinquishing the pacing to his agitated wife. "The engineering business was named after his father: Low Engineering. That remained its name for years."

"Okay." Rhia's raised hands acquiesced. "I know Alexander was quite a popular name back then, but doesn't it make you wonder if it was somehow a passed down name?"

"You mean as in Alexander 'the howevermuch' of Greywood?"

"Maybe?" Rhia grinned at his 'howevermuch', but they both knew just how many British families named a son Alexander, and knew just how spurious the conclusion might be.

He wanted the mystery solved, but he was increasingly worried about Rhia's preoccupation with her lack of success. At times, he felt she was becoming too obsessed with finding the answers and was working herself to the bone.

"Is there anyone in Australia who can verify your mother and grandfather's origins?" Rhia asked.

"What do you mean verify?"

She explained to him what she needed beyond the internet information she'd already accessed. Unfortunately, he was sure there wasn't anyone left alive in Australia who might have more information on his grandfather's origins.

"Okay," Rhia stressed, urging him to pay closer attention. "You know the story so far. Listen again because maybe you'll detect something I've failed to pick up."

He stifled a smile. When Rhia was perturbed and intent over things like this she was like a wriggly little terrier with a particularly recalcitrant bone.

He didn't dare laugh though, since she was in serious full flow.

He was entranced by her dedication to the job she'd undertaken since she wouldn't allow him to pay her more than her usual fee rates for what she was doing at Greywood Hall, not the double salary he'd originally stipulated.

It had caused friction between them but she had been adamant about it. She wasn't paying anything for rent or food, and she accepted that he was buying the special clothes she needed, so there was no way she was accepting double salary for a job she loved doing.

"Okay, back to poor Bethany. And she was getting really poor by the way."

He nodded his agreement because he knew only too well what the upkeep of an estate like this would have been like.

"I've managed to go through the estate records, I found in the library…"

Catching her by the waist he pinned her down onto the sofa. Her wanderings were making him sea-sick.

"Sit at peace for a while woman, and tell me your story before I throw up or need a neck brace."

Rhia playfully punched his arm. "Cheeky beggar. Do you know just how much you pace?"

His answer was a quick kiss; just enough to tide him over till her update was done.

"By the way, did you know the current estate records are held by the local solicitor?"

"Sure," he answered. "The lawyer has been outsourcing the estate finances to a land management firm for years. They deal with the monies that are involved in the leasing of the Home Farm and the rented properties like your cottage. Those have paid for the maintenance of the rentals and other simple sundries. That stays the same till I become the official legal owner. Haven't I told you that before?"

"Probably."

Rhia cuddled into him as she marshalled her thoughts together. "Right then, back to Bethany. Her sources of income dried up quite quickly, especially since I've noticed that during the late 1920s, during the depression years, the estate rents were waived. You might think in the grand scheme of things rents from a few cottages wouldn't make any great difference but you'd be wrong. The rents from the Home Farm, and all the other more outlying farms and smallholdings, which at that time still belonged to the estate, had the same payment-suspended deal. For three whole years."

"That would have been a huge loss of income," he agreed, finding that quite a piece of information because it certainly made no business sense to have done it. "Back then the farm rents would have formed the bulk of the estate finances."

"I know. But remember, the depression years were horrendous. It seems to have been Bethany's way of keeping people on the estate. She still needed lots of manual labour from them."

"Did their wages dry up too?"

"No. She seems to have managed to keep paying that. There were no rises of course, but she maintained the same payment as in the early 1920s."

"So that's when more treasures started to be sold?" he guessed.

"Absolutely. Selling Greywood's resources was her way to keep the wolf from the door."

"How do you know this?"

Rhia's soft doe brown eyes filled with a sudden rush of tears, tears that hovered but didn't fall. There was no way he was going to miss the emotion that surged through her. She gripped him tightly, hugging him fiercely as she continued.

"She must have been the loneliest woman in the universe, Luke. Her diaries for those years are unbelievably heart-breaking; except of course when she mentioned your Amelia who was a very, very well-loved little girl."

She'd taken to emphasizing the words your Amelia and he found he actually looked forward to it peppering her conversation. It gave him a sense of…place, a sense of real ownership, which was stupid because he still wasn't the clear and outright owner of the property.

"You're making fantastic progress with the research, Rhia, but your findings still don't explain why I was made the beneficiary?"

"No, so far I can't unravel that last detail. I'm beginning to think you need to get a private detective onto the case."

Rhia didn't know that he had long considered that himself but, although curious about being willed

Greywood Hall, he hadn't quite wanted to stir up skeletons in his own family closets. He was astute enough to realise that the indications were that something was amiss.

Rhia continued, "Did Amelia Greywood's lawyer ever hint at all why you were the beneficiary?"

"No. But remember at the time I found out about the will, the local lawyer was out of the country on holiday, and his work was in the hands of one of his juniors."

"So, maybe if I contacted the older lawyer he might have something we've yet to know?"

He took her hands between his own and squeezed comfortingly. "No problem with trying Rhia, but don't get your hopes up." He kissed her, not a compensatory kiss, but just because he needed to whenever she was close by. "I admit that once I got onto the whole bandwagon of getting you on board, and what with our wedding to arrange, and moving up the business office to this area, I never thought to ask for an appointment with the older lawyer when he returned from his holiday."

Rhia was distracted from her task when he lifted her onto his knees and proceeded to do what he felt he did pretty well. No more talk of his inheritance surfaced that night.

The next morning, however, it came as no surprise when Rhia told him she was popping into the nearest town, having made an emergency appointment with the older lawyer. The answers the man gave her were intriguing.

He hadn't suddenly become the beneficiary of a new will. For years he'd always been named as prime recipient in earlier versions of Amelia's will though substantial revisions had been authorised when she'd turned ninety, the year before Amelia's death. Adjustments were made to the small bequests for her carers since there was almost no capital left in the bank: the expenses of living at Beechlee Nursing Home had eaten well into any remaining cash resources, the rents from the leased land only barely covering her medical costs and basic repairs to the leased properties. She'd apparently, and extremely reluctantly, gone to Beechlee because she was wheelchair bound. The cost of her care and general living at home in Greywood Hall had been astronomical. Yet though infirm of body, her mind had been sharp till her death.

There was one particular clause concerning him that had been altered the year before Amelia died.

"I'm not sure how to tell you," Rhia's voice faltered when she updated him at lunchtime. "I can hardly believe it but the lawyer's information clarifies that Amelia always knew you were living in Australia." He winced at that piece of new information. "She had you added as the main beneficiary nine weeks after your birth…so somehow, she always knew of your existence."

He was just as astounded as she said she had been. "What was the thing that concerned me then? That she changed a year ago?"

"She changed the condition of you residing in Greywood Hall with your spouse, but the lawyer won't reveal any more to me. He's prepared to give you more, though, if you contact him."

Incensed wasn't too strong a word for how he felt when he ended the call. "Amelia's lawyer tells me that the original bequest had no mention of me living with a spouse at Greywood till about a year ago. This was apparently because, about five years ago, she had initiated a private investigator to check my marital and financial status. For the following four years, she had a yearly update on that."

He stomped about the room exasperated by the information he'd just learned. "The friggin'…woman knew exactly how I was fixed financially speaking, and that I obviously had no intention of getting married. The gall of her. What right did she have to dictate my marital status?"

Rhia seemed stunned, and somehow hurt. "Well, we have irrefutable evidence that she knew about you, but we still have to prove how she knew. I've searched everything

I can find here. The answers definitely lie in Australia, Luke.”

“I have no intentions of travelling to Australia just now. There’s nothing pressing that can’t be handled by my managers.” He raked his fingers through his hair, a futile attempt to calm his blistering anger as he whirled away from her intent stare. “Forget about the damned legacy! Amelia obviously wanted me to have the place, so that’s that.”

“You want to stop our agreement?”

When he turned back, he couldn’t miss that Rhia’s faced had blanched to a sickly grey. “No. Of course the arrangement still stands. There’s plenty for you to work on. You can even make a start on that book you threatened to write about Amelia, compiled from her diaries.”

Before the inheritance mystery had reared its ugly head he had happily visited Brisbane every couple of months to check up on his Australian businesses, but now he found plenty of solutions to prevent the need to fly over to Australia.

He constantly told himself that he was keeping faith with the terms of Amelia’s will about residence in Yorkshire, reluctant to admit to himself that he just liked living at Greywood with Rhia. Everything was centred very efficiently around residing there. He couldn’t picture a day passing without her constant companionship, amazed that he enjoyed her camaraderie. Hell! He even liked their occasional disagreements, and there had been plenty of those since Rhia could be quite dogmatic if she thought herself to be in the right. Making up after their conflicts of opinion was a joy.

He resolutely refused to consider, at that point, what he was going to do with the property when it eventually, legally became his.

Greywood was creeping into his heart; it was becoming a home that he actually liked to live in for the first time in his whole life. He really liked the notion that Rhia was always somewhere around and he could intercept her frequently when he needed to make contact with her, or snatch a quick kiss during the work day.

Although a confirmed workaholic and he continued to be that, he squeezed in opportunities several times a day just to touch base with her.

Rhia was in his system.

More than seven months into their cohabitation things began to unravel. For the first time since their marriage he had to spend one night in London without Rhia accompanying him since she'd picked up a disgusting cold, followed by a persistent chest infection, and still wasn't well enough to travel.

On his return the following evening he swept her into his arms and kissed her cheek soundly because she had turned her cracked lips away from him just in time. He was distressed to find she was still under the weather, her cough rattling like mad, but he had the very thing tucked away in his pocket.

After a very theatrical flourish, he gave her a beautiful white gold amethyst pendant with matching bracelet and earrings.

"To cheer you up."

"I don't need jewellery, Luke." Rhia croaked, handing the set back to him.

It was grossly unfair of her to take her mood out on him, but he could see how miserable she was feeling. Any amusement vanished when her next retort blasted out.

"Take them back and get a refund. Jewellery isn't in our agreement!"

An attempt to soften her nasty comment failed, even though she told him afterwards that she was touched that he'd thought about her and had taken time out of his work filled schedule to buy the gift. She was shrewish over the incredible expense and even cast suspicion over his purpose.

"It makes me feel like someone who has to be thrown a bone to keep her happy. I don't want them, Luke."

In her present mood he couldn't persuade her otherwise, her vehement reaction to the gift creating tension between them.

"I wanted to cheer you up," he protested. "My first proper gift and you throw it back in my face. I wish I'd never bothered."

A week later they went to an awards function in central London. The ceremony was graced by the wealthy and worthy. He was delighted with how Rhia coped at the events he sometimes felt were a necessary chore. Her natural humour and candour endeared her to his colleagues and contacts. Her natural beauty meant she looked spectacular especially when gowned and glittered like she was that night.

She'd come back earlier that day from a brief shopping trip totally enthused by the fact she'd bagged a tremendous bargain: a gorgeous gown at half price, her enthusiasm infectious. He was still amazed that she always thought so carefully about spending his money for special events. His unique wife. She was stunning in the simply styled deep purple sheath, a piece of heavy silk that fit to perfection, the cowl neckline revealing just enough cleavage to make it enticing and not brash.

Luke went to the small wall safe and withdrew the amethyst jewellery set that had caused such dissention the previous week.

"This will match your gown perfectly, Rhia. I'd love to see you wear these tonight. Will you? For me?"

She gave in.

After he had fastened the clasp of the pendant he curved his arms around her, and hugged her fiercely tight. Italian endearments dripped off his tongue. No placebo, he really meant them.

"You look absolutely stunning in that gown, and I want to rip it off you right now, but we're late."

"Taxi's already waiting for us." He loved Rhia's playful nudge before she sauntered to the door.

Resplendent in their finery, he mingled with Rhia at his side. While speaking with some acquaintances of his before dinner, a strident female voice interrupted the conversation, making him turn.

"Good evening, Luke. Isn't the time passing rapidly, my darling?"

He cringed, silently cursing a blue streak as the glamorous red-head leaned in with both hands at his cheeks, not to give a typical air kiss, but to place her lips deliberately on his for a lingering kiss. Luke was stunned at her audacity and was slow to disengage from her. He'd never wanted to meet up with Danielle ever again, but here she was as bold as brass and stirring mischief as only she could do.

When he removed Danielle's hands from his cheeks, he watched her eyes flick condescendingly over Rhia's appearance before she returned her heated gaze to him. The bitching tone that followed was one he'd never expected to hear again.

"Do you know I think that amethyst trifling actually does look a little bit better on her, my darling. But then, you were also correct that diamonds are so much better suited to me."

Danielle performed an insolent bow in front of Rhia before drifting off; her heavy perfume lingering long after her high-couture-clad body had gone. Luke could swear Rhia's feet were welded to the floor, her legs being so rigid with tension. Her instant white alarmed him.

No…more than that it terrified him.

He excused them from their companions and dragged Rhia to a quiet part of the room. "Are you all right?" He was so angry he could barely speak.

"Danielle?" Rhia numbly asked, her eyes pools of misery as she strove for composure, self-control he could see was hard won. "How could I possibly mistake that voice?"

"Yes, that's Danielle," he answered but ventured no further explanation. "If you're feeling unwell, we'd better just leave." He yanked out his cell phone out to summon a taxi.

"No!" Rhia stopped his call, her hand over the phone. "I'm fine. It's far too early to go and the awards haven't even started yet. You have to be here for the one you're hoping to receive."

He was being given an award for a reconstruction project he'd done a couple of years previously on an almost derelict estate. Though not the most prestigious award that evening, he knew he should be there to accept it, but he wished them a million miles away from the harpy named Danielle.

***

For the next hour Rhia tried to appear happy to be by Luke's side, but her insecurity ate away at her confidence and made her unusually silent and less responsive. What could Danielle's cryptic words mean? Time passing quickly? Her diamonds?

What was that all about?

She knew Luke was displeased with her withdrawal, and his persistent concern about her wellbeing was beginning to grate. His present solicitousness didn't make her any happier about her longer term situation. Though she was desperately in love with him, he'd never ever told her he loved her.

For the second time in their relationship she felt used.

In the ladies cloakroom, just before they left, that vicious voice intruded again. Danielle's image towered over her own in the mirror as Rhia washed her hands, far too close for comfort.

"I hope you like Luke's choice of jewellery," Danielle purred. "He wanted me to have that set at first because they're such distinctive designer originals, but I much prefer diamonds." Her hands fluttered to her neck and fingered the huge solitaire that sparkled there. "They suit my colouring so much better. But I hope that every time you wear those paltry amethysts you'll think of me wearing this."

Danielle's bray trilled out again sending ice cool draughts down Rhia's spine. "But it doesn't worry me overmuch that you have that little trinket. Luke will buy me much more expensive jewellery in the future – that is, after he's got shot of you."

Her exit was too swift for Rhia to summon any retaliation. She removed the amethyst jewellery and jammed it into her clutch bag before donning her serape to go out to join Luke.

"What the hell happened in there?" Luke demanded when she reached him.

"Nothing that matters." She didn't want to talk. She didn't even want to look at him. She was just desperate to get back to the apartment.

"From the way Danielle stalked off it is quite obvious there was some mudslinging. Tell me what she said to you?"

His face was thunderous. When she refused to answer he bellowed, "Let's get out of here."

Rhia was far too depleted to give any comeback. The ride back was in total, crushingly awful silence.

In the bedroom, she readied herself for bed, her heart heavy, her mind numb. Luke's anger had abated a bit but his earlier solicitous concern had returned and she felt smothered.

"I'm fine Luke, can't you get that? I'm exhausted. I just need to sleep."

For the first time in their now quite long acquaintance, she turned her back on him. One week had passed since Luke had returned with the now detested amethysts that Danielle claimed were originally intended for her. What did the ghastly woman mean? Had she and Luke spent that evening together? And more importantly what did she still mean to Luke? Did Luke and Danielle really intend to resume their relationship after he took possession of Greywood Hall like Danielle had alluded to?

She woke with the dawn light creeping in through the drapes; snuggled into Luke's embrace, still wanting him.

They spent three days in London. Three very cool days: and nothing to do with the weather. By the third day she'd come to a decision. Someone as reptilian as Danielle would not compel her to renege on her word. If staying with Luke for the whole year was going to destroy her sanity then that's what would happen because Danielle would not make her wimp out on her deal.

Chapter Thirteen

"Bloody Hell!"

Rhia was drawing back from him and Luke didn't know what to do to amend it.

No matter what he tried, somehow they'd lost the fun they'd shared. Something wasn't right, but he ignored it in the hope that it would blow over. In his previous life, this would have been a turning point for him. No fun, no point. But there was no way Rhia would slide out of his life. She meant much more to him than any woman ever before. He couldn't imagine one single future day without her beside him.

He stared at his computer monitor, his concentration shot to pieces as he worked out strategies to get them back to where they were before the now-detested awards event.

There was also another problem that really needed to be addressed. Rhia was working herself into exhaustion. She pored over diaries and paperwork all day long: the negative results frustrating her since there were still no definitive facts pointing to why Amelia chose him. Her eagerness was waning. She often appeared unable to summon up enough energy or enthusiasm, but doggedly ploughed on. She was sometimes moody for no good reasons; mood swings that couldn't be put down to attacks of hormones gone wrong because it had continued for weeks. Her pallor was increasing day by day.

She'd stopped insisting that the answer to his legacy riddle would only be solved in Australia – in fact the bequest question hadn't been talked about at all for what seemed like ages.

He reluctantly concluded that only a visit to Australia would banish her depression. If Amelia had had some kind of proof that he was related to her through Jocasta, were the implications of that going to be devastating? Was he some kind of cuckoo in his parent's nest? Had he inherited both his father's and his mother's separate fortunes somehow illegally – if he wasn't actually their son?

Thinking about his inflexible attitude over visiting Australia, he realised he'd been an arrogant shit about many other things during their months together, because apart from business trips to London all they'd had for months was a lot of work, their cohabitation, and fabulous sex.

No days off or holidays.

He'd never done any of the dating rituals that he'd entered into with previous lovers. Normal courting hadn't been part of their contract. Since Rhia had never seemed to need any of that, it hadn't occurred to him that it could be an element in their relationship that was lacking. She'd always filled the cottage with flowers from her garden so he'd never bought any. Nor had he bought chocolates. They'd been far too busy restoring Greywood Hall and partaking in the extra jaunts necessary to his business.

Apart from the fiasco of the amethyst pendant set, he'd never bought her any gifts, having learned from his initial attempts that she never wanted any material things from him. In his defence, she'd made it clear they were unnecessary.

Where did it leave him, if she was now turning away?

"I've postponed the schedule for the new property in Cornwall," he declared as they prepared dinner. "Instead of Bissoe you're going to have a holiday in Brisbane instead."

"I don't want a holiday," Rhia groused, fiddling with the spoon as she swirled the pasta she was boiling. "Go yourself, if you need to check out the Brisbane office." Verbalizing all sorts of reasons why he should go himself, she carried on with their meal preparations, totally avoiding eye-contact. "You can ask all the necessary questions just as well as me." Her voice was of the no holds barred variety that he knew meant business. "I'll make you a list before you go."

"We'll only be away for ten days." Luke's patience was getting thinner as he set the table.

"Too long and you know it." She set out the full bowls of penne marinara on the table with a determined thud. "You know what the stipulations are."

"The lawyers have agreed it." Luke still couldn't get her to make decent eye contact. "I wouldn't be telling you about it if they hadn't."

His deadly patient tone was creating as much tension as Rhia's reticence. Neither enjoyed the dish they'd created a few times already and had thoroughly relished. Rhia twiddled her fork for one more time before she pushed her plate away as though the very sight of their concoction made her gag.

"This isn't a good time for me to be away so long. I'm almost finished cataloguing the library and it's not good to discontinue the flow."

He dropped the subject when she wouldn't back down, and because he couldn't deal with the friction it was causing between them.

Their life continued at Greywood Hall for another month with intermittent day long work jaunts, but Rhia was looking even more exhausted by the time she declared she'd completed the library cataloguing. By then Luke reasoned that taking her somewhere closer than Australia might do the trick. He arranged for them to have a surprise weekend trip.

"Rome?"

He was so glad to see her eyes were a picture of delight.

"I need to discuss the shares I inherited from my father in the Salieri import-export business. I'm considering selling, but I want to speak to my uncle Stefano first. It's easier to meet with him in Rome than it is for him to come to London. He doesn't travel as well as he used to. Ever been to Rome?"

"Me?" she squeaked. "I've never been to Italy. I've only been outside the UK when I visited my father in Brussels, and one other time when I went on a school trip to ski in Austria."

The following day they were in Italy. The welcome by his aunt and uncle was poignant for Luke: he'd not visited for some years, and their greeting was effusive. He was used to their lingering hugs and kisses but Rhia wasn't – her high colour evidence of her discomfort. His uncle spoke excellent English, his elderly aunt less well but Luke was aware of her efforts to make Rhia feel comfortable since he had explained that Rhia had only studied French at school.

They dined at a nearby restaurant that evening. His other uncle and aunt came, along with several cousins and their spouses, and as many other extended family as could join them at such short notice.

Luke knew it was quite daunting for Rhia to cope with his boisterous Italian relatives. The older adults were very formal in their approach to her but the ones of contemporary age were eager to learn details of how and when Luke had met her. Most of them spoke pretty good English.

He was impressed when Rhia gave them a credible version of the truth; entertaining them with the true story of her having him arrested by the police at Greywood Hall. He was surprised by her creativity – it sounded so plausible as she explained it.

It had been love at first sight when they'd shared the back of the police patrol car. Their love had spiralled from that first day, their marriage coming a scant two weeks after. He'd happily gone along with her version for his relatives' sakes, wondering just how possible her tale could be.

Could she have fallen in love with him that first day? Her recently cool attitude belied it.

He still wasn't sure what love was, but he did know he lusted after Rhia just as much as he had that first day…and honestly admitted to himself that he didn't think that was ever going to change. He really liked daily living with her, sharing Greywood and all its trials and tribulations and he was very concerned over her welfare.

He happily translated when needed, but that wasn't too often. The younger women were chatty and friendly: some of the men were flirty.

He jealously fended off a few unattached male cousins of his whose attentions to Rhia were just a little too assiduous for his liking.

The evening passed in a blur of conversation peppered with invitations to join in with other planned family occasions in the future. Rhia was struggling to answer; her delicate colouring alerted him to her discomfiture so he replied for both of them.

Seven and a half weeks? Was that all? After that, Rhia would no longer be bound to him. She'd be able to leave Greywood and…do what? Live alone in the cottage? With him living alone at Greywood? Till he sold it and moved on?

Could he sell Greywood now that he'd done so much there?

Only seven and a half weeks?

No wonder Rhia was flustered about accepting the invitations from his family. The fact hung heavy on his heart. He'd put Rhia into an unbearable situation yet again, but she endured it with her inherent silent fortitude. It hit home that, over recent weeks, she'd also tactfully sidestepped invitations issued by colleagues and friends back in England. She always used their hectic work schedules as an excuse.

His family's total acceptance of her as his wife sat heavily on his conscience, for in normal circumstances she'd fit in extremely well with them.

Hell's Bells!

She did fit in.

"Your uncles and other family are lovely people, Luke," Rhia said when they were back in the guest suite of his uncle's villa and getting ready for bed. "Was your father like your uncles?"

He yanked off his shirt and threw it onto the back of a chair before answering, his throat feeling tight. "Not at all. He was nothing like them." He was aware of Rhia's eyes tracking him as he unhurriedly drew his belt through the loops of his trousers, and then she flinched when he summarily slapped it down on the floor. "He favoured my uncle Roberto in looks, but his personality was nothing like any of my Italian relatives. They're lovely warm people. He wasn't."

He was more than aware that his last statement said a lot about his relationship with his father but Rhia knew better than to intervene when he recalled unhappy childhood memories, knew just how much talking about his parents always put him in a bad mood.

"My father had none of their charm or warmth." He slumped down on the bed to remove his shoes and socks. "Well, at least not for me."

He knew his laugh was full of bitter undertones but he was at pains to prevent it.

"My esteemed father could be very charming to women in his company, but he never ever wanted to be shackled to a growing boy. If I didn't favour my Italian relatives in looks, especially my father since I'm said to be his clone, I'd be thinking that the sperm to produce me came from someone else."

Rhia was silent as she lay on the bed, yet how could he expect her to respond when he'd just disclosed such a revelation.

"But if my father was cold, he was like the blazing sun compared to my darling mother, who barely tolerated me. Oh, she trotted me out for her women friends to admire, then patted my head and sent me back to the nursery."

His body hit the sheets where he lay rigid. "I've told you that at aged seven going on eight, I was shipped off to

England to begin my education in the best prep schools. After that it was Cambridge University."

He reached for Rhia's hand as he continued in fits and starts – drowning in past memories. "During those years in exile…"

His terminology earned him a tighter grip from Rhia's fingers. "My mother always managed to make sure I spent lots of holiday time in England or in Europe with parents of boys who were at school with me. Or the boys came to our house in Australia to be supervised by my current nanny – a nanny engaged for that time only – for why on earth would she employ the same one all year while I was away?"

He was so wrapped up in his lonely recollections that at first he scarcely felt Rhia's gentle stroking. Her fingers soothed his temples and massaged his chest where his heart thumped.

"Sometimes she shipped me off to my uncles here in Italy to improve my Italian, which was unnecessary because my father insisted that some of the nannies be Italian, so I was as fluent as I could be."

He shifted onto his side to take her into his arms and to look into her so very compassionate eyes.

"I always knew my mother resented having to arrange for me. I was a reminder of the biggest mistake of her life." His arms squeezed her into a tighter embrace, his head buried into her neck.

"I can't quite remember all of the details." Rhia's whisper was tentative. "Were you born soon after your parents married?"

His grim laugh echoed in the room before he relaxed a little for the first time in minutes. "Strangely enough the answer is no. I was born a couple of years after they married. But they were always so formal with each other that I never ever knew if they loved each other even a little bit at the beginning."

There was a tense silence for a few seconds. Then Luke opened the floodgates and let the fetid acid flush out of his system, knowing he'd never divulged so much about his parents to anyone ever before.

"My father strayed a lot, although he was always discreet. My mother turned a blind eye." The exhalation of his breath fluttered Rhia's hair as he clutched her even more tightly. Confident that she knew it for what it was, his search was for solace. "To my knowledge my mother never had any extra marital liaisons, but she was so efficient I guess it was possible and I never found out."

"Were your parents never close at all during your childhood?"

"Not so far as I could ever tell, but remember I was hardly at home." He idly stroked her hair with loving touches. "They had separate bedrooms in the huge mansion where we lived. They weren't adjoining. In actual fact they existed in separate wings of the house." His lips caressed her brow. "I lived in a third wing with whatever nanny was on duty at the time." He absently stroked Rhia's back. "The fourth wing was strictly for guests. Mother had a lot of those, mainly women of her acquaintance. Father rarely had guests. At least while I was home."

When he squeezed her in a tighter grip he realised Rhia was squirming away from him. Angry at her rejection, he whipped onto his back and drew in deep breaths.

"People should never have children if they aren't going to love them. I hate the idea of bringing children into this world!" He pulled up the bedcover and turned his back on Rhia, angry with himself for offloading his family grief. She was the only person in the world he could ever talk to but she'd shied from his embrace.

Remaining on his side, he bid her goodnight. He had just wanted her comfort.

Sleep was long in coming that night.

They were both good at pretence next morning; it was as though the revelations had never caused a rift. They played tourist: Luke leading Rhia on a whirlwind tour of sights around Rome. By late morning, he had made up his mind. He was going to win back the easy relationship they'd had.

At every opportunity he held her hand; stroked her back if they were queuing; casually slung his arm across her shoulders keeping her close. All were gestures which Rhia seemed to love and happily reciprocated but which confused him even more.

Why could she allow his touch out in public but not in the confines of their bed?

He couldn't decide whether the visit to his relatives had been a success, or not. He'd never introduced any other woman to them before, nor had he ever wanted to. He acknowledged he wanted to include Rhia in all aspects of his family life, which included information about his less than salubrious time with his parents. He'd never divulged so many family secrets before.

She'd loved visiting the tourist spots, a spark of her natural enthusiasm returning for those all too short hours, her genuine smiles warming him to the core. He was certain she'd enjoyed meeting his Italian family, but there was a sadness that he still couldn't explain.

He was convinced he'd been right to drag her over to Rome, but was she wishing that the few weeks left of their contract were already over?

***

Rhia wasn't just going through the motions of honouring their contract. She wasn't disinterested in visiting Italy or Australia, or in pursuing his family history.

It had eventually become clear why she'd been feeling off colour for some weeks. Since the persistent cough had lingered for ages, she'd thought her tiredness and nausea were a legacy of the chest infection she'd had.

"Nothing to worry about, Mrs. Salieri." Her doctor had beamed at her after asking a few initial questions and had taken simple blood and urine samples. "You'll be right as rain soon. Lots of women feel tired and out of sorts in their first stages of pregnancy. Some vitamins and folic acid will address that.”

“Pregnant? But I’ve been using contraceptives…”

“You were recently given a course of anti-biotic for a chest infection?” He read her notes on screen.

“Yes, and I took them to the end of the ten day course.”

“Sometimes the efficacy of contraceptives is affected by an anti-biotic. Weren’t you informed of that at the time?” the doctor questioned.

Rhia had to be honest. “Er…yes, I was warned to be more vigilant.”

“I’m sure your husband will be delighted with your news Mrs. Salieri.”

She stumbled out on auto-pilot, a prescription crushed in her hand. Pregnancy was no part of their bargain. How on earth could she tell Luke?

The time clock on their agreement was ticking to a close and they only had a few weeks left of their agreement.

Rhia took no time at all to make up her mind about the pregnancy. She would have the child regardless of how Luke felt about being a father. Guilt lay heavy on her shoulders because she was the one who’d encouraged their love making sessions during those vulnerable days in London after the Danielle fiasco.

If she went away before the year was up, without telling him about her pregnancy, then he’d not own Greywood and that was what it was all about. And it was so beautifully restored now it would break her heart to have it go out of his ownership.

“Greywood?” she cried to no one in particular when she was out walking Thor in the woods after her visit to the doctor. “How can I sabotage your future?” She’d no earthly idea what would happen to the estate if she, and Luke, didn’t fulfil their residence terms.

Luke had never told her he loved her, or that he wanted their unorthodox relationship to continue beyond the stipulated year.

For another whole week she worried herself sick over the problem, finding no immediate solution. Luke knew she was taking vitamins and supplements. At first she had been horrified when he'd noticed them in her toilet bag but when she realised he was delighted she'd sought help to improve her health, she abhorred lying to him.

Omitting to tell him seemed just the same.

The issue over a trip to Australia caused problems again. He declared a visit to sort out business concerns was essential.

"I told you before; you can ask all the questions yourself, Luke!" Tension was so great she felt she'd probably lost some tooth enamel. "I don't need to go and I don't want to go."

"I have to," he insisted. "Where I go…you go. You know the rules."

The postscript he added was the clincher. "And anyway you know too bloody well this stupid problem of my inheritance must be resolved before it kills you. We're leaving on Saturday."

In two days.

She'd never asked the Rentons to look after Thor for more than one night, but this visit was going to be for much longer than that. Prepared to put him in kennels for the duration, even though the thought made her really nervous, she phoned June Renton to say they'd not need to look after Thor that week since there would be no weekly London visit. Her relief could not have been greater when June insisted it would be a pleasure to look after the dog till they returned.

After that, all she had to do was sort herself out for long haul flights. She had never had morning sickness as such. During those weeks of feeling off-colour, she'd learned a few techniques to keep any queasiness at bay and continued to employ them during their travels.

On arrival in Brisbane, they immediately went to Luke's parents' house.

"Why did you just mothball the house?" Rhia asked as he drove a hired car to the expensive Brisbane suburb. "What made you keep it all this time?"

He took a few moments to answer her. She didn't think the delay had anything to do with the light traffic on the road that he was accounting for. His tone was pretty indifferent.

"I guess I just never wanted to even spend the time it would have taken to get the estate agents on board and organise the sale."

His response sounded lame, and Rhia knew him well enough to realise that wasn't the full answer.

As they drove up a very impressive curving driveway Rhia's whispered, "No use me guessing. I suppose that this is prime, hugely expensive property and a great addition to your investment portfolio?"

"You could say that," Luke chuckled and then added, "It was easiest to keep it in the care of mother's housekeeper and her husband, who is the general handyman. They'd been with mother all my life and I suppose I've kept it on for them more than for any other reason."

She smiled as she nudged his arm, "So it was for sentimental reasons you big jerk!"

He brought the car to a halt and parked. "Meg and Andy were almost the grandparents I'd never met, and they've been the most constant thing in my life. I always came home at holiday time to a new nanny…but it was Meg's arms that hugged me at the door."

It was a handsome old property. As a student of history and architecture she could appreciate its design and the ornate styles of interior decorating which Luke's mother had established. It had very quaint English touches throughout but it was formally ornamented and was utterly characterless for a family home.

"It's lovely, Luke," she mumbled after a warm greeting from Meg and Andy, who as Luke had predicted had welcomed them at the front door. The couple had then left them to it after Luke asked for coffee in the library as soon as possible.

"Liar!" Luke grinned. "It's the most uncomfortable place you can imagine. But no worries, Meg won't be offended. If she shows you their little house in the grounds you'll see the cosy retreat I escaped to whenever I could."

It wasn't a place Rhia could imagine a child growing up in. Not like Greywood Hall now was and probably had been centuries before.

Once they'd deposited their suitcases and Luke had given her a very dispassionate whistle-stop guided tour of the whole house – all four wings built around a central patio courtyard – they settled for some coffee in the library. It was a grandiose room with an extensive mahogany desk and two high walls of books. The other two walls were crammed with photographs of people and places. Browsing around the framed photographic collection she gasped as she made a more than interesting discovery.

"Luke?" She ran towards him, excitement propelling her feet as she groped for his hand to drag him back to where she'd just been. "I can't credit this."

She was equally excited when Luke jumped up and twirled her around, crushing her close, showing his own thrill.

"My old Rhia's back! " His eager kiss told her just how pleased he was, but she pulled out of his clutches and dragged him over to the photographs she'd been looking at.

"Have you ever looked at these?" She tripped over her words.

"According to my mother, they're family, friends and business acquaintances," Luke's smile showed his delight in her enthusiasm.

"Is there some kind of record of who they might be?" she asked, wondering if he would think her question odd.

"Darn right there is! My mother was a stickler for that sort of thing."

The twinkle in his eyes and his quirky smile meant he was dead set on teasing her. Rhia had seen that look plenty of times over the past almost-year! But she played his game, a little, since she needed answers. She allowed one more kiss, then pulled away again.

"You're no fun, Rhia," Luke complained though she knew he wasn't serious. "Okay" he smiled, "You win. For now."

He looked at the rows of photographs as though he needed to remind himself of the information she sought, then caught her unexpectedly around the waist and twirled her in circles. "The names, my darling dogged little terrier, are likely to all be on the back."

"On the back?" She pointed to one particular photograph, blinking hard at his use of 'darling'. Usually endearments were in Italian. Quelling the flutter of hope his word stirred, she made herself sound merely excited by her question. "Would you mind if we opened up this one to see who this woman is?" She indicated one particular old Edwardian sepia photograph.

When Luke removed the back clips of the expensive frame and extracted the photograph he inhaled sharply. Jocasta Greywood.

"How on earth did you know?" he asked, "We've barely been in this room for ten minutes."

"Can't you see the likeness?" Rhia giggled at his amazement. "She looks exactly like the woman on the horse in the dining room painting at Greywood Hall." She chuckled again, amazed that a connection with Greywood was so out in the open.

Luke slumped into a chair beside her, reverently holding the photograph.

"But my mother redecorated this whole library less than a year before she died. She had everything reframed at vast expense, according to my father, who grumbled about the inconvenience at the time. The money for matching reframing was peanuts, but this room was always his sanctuary, his personal retreat. He hated anyone even in here to dust it when his paperwork was strewn all over that very desk.”

“Is this your mother’s writing? Or someone else’s?” She displayed the back of the photograph.

“Definitely my mother’s,” Luke confirmed, getting angrier as he worked through the implications. “But that would mean she was familiar with the name Jocasta Greywood. She must have known the Greywood Hall connection and never ever breathed a word of it.”

Chapter Fourteen

"My mother's lawyer must have had the originals, or at the very least copies," Luke reasoned, "I never had anything to do with them when my mother's will was read."

Although his mother had been an extremely organised person, on searching her personal domain in the mansion Rhia hadn't found any important documents. There was no trace of his mother's Birth Certificate or her Marriage Certificate. That seemed strange even to him.

"And your father's?"

"By the time my father died, he'd already removed all his personal documentation to Italy," he told her, but over the following two days they searched every wing of the house, just in case.

Rhia set in motion a thorough search through the Australian Records system, much more detailed than she'd been able to access from England. She paged through local Church Parish registers, and other official sources, and found more success.

It took three days of extensive searching to find the details of his mother's connections to Jocasta Greywood, during which time he went to his Brisbane office and caught up with business. Although she was again working herself to the bone, she was energized by the excitement of her findings. Her verve was back: he commented that he couldn't be more delighted.

Eventually what she found explained the mystery of Greywood Hall.

"On arrival in Australia, Jocasta Greywood was pregnant – father unknown – but she'd conceived during her sojourn in Italy," she explained, showing him the evidence she'd printed.

"But why would she have come to Australia?" he wanted to know.

Her answer was conjectural. "Maybe she was too embarrassed to return to Greywood Hall as an unmarried mother…or perhaps the father was an Australian national and she'd followed him here."

Purely speculative reasons with not a shred of evidence to confirm it.

"But look at this, Luke."

She was once again so excited with her local sleuthing. He took the slip of paper she held out. "This is the Australian Records Department copy of the birth."

He was confused as he read it. "But this is for Alexander Low."

Rhia laughed at his puzzled expression. "Yes, it is. And this is why I couldn't make the connection back in England. But don't worry, there's more to tell you – this isn't Alexander's original birth record."

Still an unmarried mother, Jocasta gave birth to an illegitimate son she named Alexander Grey Wood, registering the name Wood for a surname.

"Why would she do that?" He couldn't fathom Jocasta's reasoning for doing it.

"I'm guessing she was still mortified about registering an illegitimate son with her proper name. Or maybe it was a genuine mistake, as sometimes happened when registering births. Or maybe because she was in a different country, she thought to conceal it."

Archived local newspaper sources of the time confirmed that before her son Alexander was two years old Jocasta married a much older man named David Low. David Low was a manufacturing giant in Brisbane at the time and articles featured him and his family for many years after their marriage.

Rhia's searches had revealed that Alexander had been officially adopted after Jocasta's marriage to David Low, and his surname changed. She had discovered the details from adoption records in Brisbane; records not available to her in England. A completely new birth certificate subsequently registered Low as his surname, the old one expunged from the official records.

"Was that usual?"

"Normal practice in England would have been to amend an original birth record with changed circumstances."

Rhia explained that during her earliest searches at Greywood she had been working on the assumption that Australian documentation would have been similarly altered. Months before, all she had been able to authenticate had been a birth record for an Alexander Low – not Greywood.

Why a totally new certificate had been created and the first destroyed seemed highly irregular…but it answered the mystery.

"This is why I couldn't work out the connections from England." Rhia sounded both chuffed that she'd found the irrefutable proof but also frustrated and annoyed that she'd not been able to access the critical details from Greywood Hall.

He learned that since Jocasta and David had had no other children, Alexander had become the heir to David Low's engineering firm. Rhia could find nothing to prove that David Low might, in fact, have been Alexander's biological father, but he certainly had brought the boy up as his own son.

In due time Alexander married, and his wife gave birth to Luke's mother in 1935, their only child. They had called her Elizabeth Lucy Low.

"Lucy? I didn't know mother had a middle name," Luke questioned. "Do you think that might have been a diminutive of Lucinda?"

"Could be, and perhaps Luke is also sort of Greywood name?" Rhia added.

"No, I don't think so. Remember that my recorded birth name is the Italian Lucca, not Luke."

"But what's to say your mother didn't influence that choice? Maybe she wanted the closest Italian to a Greywood name?"

It was good reasoning, but unfortunately they'd never know.

Luke was disgusted when he realised his mother must always have known the Greywood family history, yet chose not to tell him. But why? Maybe because Brisbane society didn't tolerate infringements to normal patterns of behaviour, and she had been such a sticker for social acceptance.

From doing another thorough search of his mother's wing of the mansion, he and Rhia eventually found one particular letter that gave their theories credence.

Tucked into a novel in the little bedside bookcase in his mother's bedroom, it had remained unopened for years. It was an official lawyer's letter clearly labelled to Lucca Salieri and had been sent on behalf of Amelia Greywood of Greywood Hall in Yorkshire. The missive confirmed that Luke would inherit Greywood Hall when Amelia died.

It was dated twelve years before, just prior to when he had turned twenty one.

"How could my mother not have told me about this, Rhia?"

She comforted him, her empathy unrestrained. It was only when Rhia asked Meg, the housekeeper, if she could add any details that other surprising revelations were made.

Rhia persuaded Meg to come and talk to him.

"I'm so sorry, Luke. You know I'd never ever want to hurt you but perhaps you should hear everything I've kept secret for far too long."

He hated seeing Meg so distressed. "It's definitely time you shared whatever it is, Meg, since it seems too great a burden."

"It isn't good to speak ill of the dead, Luke, but I was your mother's housekeeper for nearly twenty five years before she dropped like a stone. I saw many things I'd rather not have."

He urged Meg to sit on one of the couches and knelt at her knees, like he had done so many times as a young boy. "Please tell me everything. I need to know who I am, and everything about the mother who gave birth to me, Meg."

Meg nodded, her lips quivering as she held back her tears, but the small loving smile she always had for him was mirrored in her glistening eyes. She inhaled deeply through her nose before speaking. "Your mother died of a massive heart attack one week before your twenty-first birthday. Elizabeth refused to tell your father, or you, that she'd had heart problems for some time before that. She told me, since I'd seen her medication in her bathroom, but Elizabeth swore me to secrecy. Her sudden death devastated your father because it was only then that he found out that, for a couple of years, the family doctor had been advising your mother to ease her working day."

Luke swore. In robust Italian. "How could she do that? She was always a selfish bitch!"

His temper only subsided a little when he felt Rhia unclench the fist he had just pummelled against the cushion next to Meg's knee, her hand wrapping around his in solidarity as she knelt beside him. Her quiet question to Meg made him focus more on his housekeeper's distress rather than his own.

"It was so long ago, but can you tell us anything about the letter that arrived, Meg?"

Meg managed a weak chuckle. "Not so long ago, Rhia. Luke's still a young man."

After a short pause to think about it the housekeeper continued. "The letter must have arrived just shortly before she died. Elizabeth's business correspondence always went to her company office, but it was a rare day that your mother didn't have a personal mail delivery here. She had lots of friends who sent her letters and invitations." At that, Meg burst into a flood of gulping tears that she tried to suppress.

He waited a moment till Meg managed to compose herself. "Was it usual for my mother to tuck letters into books?" He'd never seen his mother do it but truth to tell, he didn't actually know his mother's habits.

Wiping away her tears with a tissue that Rhia produced, Meg sniffed. "I've dusted her bookcases regularly, Luke, but envelopes inside the books aren't something I've ever noticed. After her death, I definitely cleaned her rooms and tidied away anything Elizabeth had left lying around so I may have put that particular book away." Her finger shaking, she pointed to the one that had contained the envelope before her gaze sought his and held. "Maybe Elizabeth planned to tell you about it when you came home from America, but she never got the chance?"

Now Luke would never know. He patted Meg's hand and gently caressed her fingers when more silent tears started to fall.

"I'm wondering why your father never found this Luke, when he went through your mother's things?"

Rhia's careful question distracted him as he moved up to sit alongside Meg on the settee. He stretched his arm across Meg's shoulders and pulled the older woman into a gentle hug.

"Father didn't do anything at all with any of mother's personal belongings." Luke knew his tone was as flat as a pancake but didn't care to do anything about it. "Remember Rhia, I told you that they lived in their different wings of the house and the saying never the twain shall meet was almost the daily norm."

"Surely he must have done something with her things when she died?"

"You must be joking!" From the notable flinch he knew his sarcastic laugh had hurt Rhia, though he didn't mean it to. "After mother's death, my father couldn't sell up his own Australian based import and export business quickly enough. Within five weeks he went back to Italy to stay with his brother Stefano before he bought a house for himself. He never returned to Australia. He died later that same year in a freak alpine avalanche while skiing."

Rhia seemed astounded. She looked at Meg whose gulping nod confirmed his words.

"He just upped and left you in Australia?" Rhia was shocked.

"At twenty one I was old enough to make my own way in the world. I had inherited my mother's businesses and was rolling in money. It would have been far too late for him to have been any kind of tender father to me."

He urged a now really-distressed Meg up off the settee and ushered her to the door, his attempt at consoling his housekeeper heartfelt but awkward since he could see he was making Meg's situation worse.

Rhia pulled the door open. "I'll take Meg back to her quarters, Luke. I'll not be a moment."

He walked over to the window and stared out, not seeing anything much at all. Uncovering the illegitimate skeleton in his family cupboard was more devastating than he'd bargained for. He might not be the illegitimate one, but the repercussions were still affecting him down the line. And Meg's unanticipated anguish was cutting him to the bone. Guilt sat heavily on his shoulders because her misery was way beyond anything he'd expected.

Rhia's soft hug from behind brought him back to reality. "Talk to me, Luke. Maybe I can help?"

"If I'd known ten years ago, I could have done something for Amelia Greywood," he ranted. "I could have visited her, got to know her. Hell, I could even have started to renovate Greywood Hall at that time, because I'd already amalgamated my father's financial legacy with the money I'd inherited from my mother. The only business I retained in Australia was her construction company and the increased revenues from it were skyrocketing at that time."

"Maybe your mother was waiting till you reached twenty one, but by then it was too late. Maybe she didn't think you were ready to handle the issue of Greywood properly before then?”

“Before then?” He laughed. A harsh, bitter uncompromising laugh that contrarily made him feel better. “In my mother’s eyes I was never going to be ready.”

Rhia tightened her grip on him, soothing his back with loving touches as he told her about that time of his life.

His mother had given him an ultimatum when he was only seventeen. Elizabeth had declared that to date she’d provided him with the very best English education he could ever have, and it was her intention to continue that through to university level, but that he’d also need to learn what it was to be a part of her business. He told Rhia that what followed had been the most difficult years of his life. Having been brought up with the expectations of a privileged background, his mother had then made him start from grass roots in her construction business. During every holiday he worked at the most menial of manual work before working up to managerial tasks.

“She was right in her own way, Rhia.” His laugh was sardonic. “By the age of twenty one I knew what a day’s work really meant and that work ethic has remained in me.”

“Surely that was a good thing, Luke?” Rhia reasoned, sensing that his memories were still bitter.

“You’d think so.” A harsh snort accompanied the grating of his fingers though his hair as he paced about. “Yet in my mother’s eyes I still never seemed to make the grade.”

Rhia had the temerity to intervene at one point to ask, “Did your father never ever have a say in what you were doing?”

His grunt was sarcastic.

“Not so much as I noticed. Father was never particularly interested in what I did and never seemed inclined to interfere, if it meant challenging my mother’s plans. He never ever rocked her boat.”

He recalled his twenty first birthday gift from his parents.

"They sent me to America for two months before I reached twenty one. No construction work was expected of me when I was overseas, it was just a jaunt so that I could become familiar with some main US cities like New York, San Francisco and what comes in between. I was in San Francisco when my father's message reached me to say my mother had had a heart attack."

He clutched Rhia.

"The heart attack was massive, so she was long dead before I could get back to Brisbane. She was such a cold hearted bitch."

The sympathy oozing from her made him continue. "Not loving like you are. Things like illegitimacy mattered to her, but this with Amelia Greywood was beyond the pale. Why did she leave an old lady without the relatives she needed in her old age? Amelia had to go into a nursing home. My mother and father were such cold-hearted people."

"Luke you're so easy to love, they must have loved you."

"No. They never should have had a child. I was obviously a mistake."

Rhia looked so shocked…and troubled. He felt her shivering in his arms.

"They tolerated me. They did their duty raising me. They went their own ways. It was an effort for them to even be at home for Christmas dinner." He was on a bitter roll. "Look at this magnificent house. What do you honestly see here?"

He could tell it was difficult for Rhia to answer truthfully.

"It's a beautiful place, but I wouldn't have wanted to live here as a child."

"It's a cold monument to gracious living. That's all my mother was interested in. She spent as little time here as necessary, yet do you realise that this was her own parents' home? This mausoleum was also where she was brought up!"

What could Rhia add to something that was testimony in itself? He didn't expect any answer from her; he just loved the empathy she radiated as she tolerated his rants.

"I will never ever do that to a child and that's why I'll never have one."

"Luke!" Rhia's cry was even more shocked than before.

Seeing he was now distressing Rhia, he stomped out of the room, desperate to get out of the miserable house that still held him hostage.

Having driven aimlessly around for hours, he returned to find Rhia fast asleep in one of the guest rooms. She'd chosen the one wing never occupied by any of the family. She was curled knees to chest, clutching a pillow with the streaks of tears and distress still visible on her cheeks.

He was shocked to the core. How could he have done this to the one person who mattered most to him in his entire life?

Not one individual in his past had ever mattered like Rhia did.

She stirred, immediately aware of his presence coming into the room. Before she could utter a single word he gathered her to him.

"Please forgive me? I never meant you to cry over me. I love you," he whispered, his voice breaking with remorse, "I'm sorry if I hurt you. You are everything to me. I can't wait any longer to tell you I love you. I don't want the year to end. I want you to be my wife well beyond the year."

"I can't, Luke." Her still sleepy eyes brimmed with even more tears. "I can't be the wife you want."

Luke was devastated. She didn't want him?

"I'm not going to let you go. I won't give you a divorce at the end of the year." He was adamant, grasping her close to him.

She struggled off the bed, her cries hysterical. "No. You have to divorce me. I won't trap you into marriage when our child is born. You'll hate our child and then you'll hate me too."

Luke sprinted after her into the hallway and halted her frantic flight.

"Our child? What do you mean I'll hate our child?"

"I'm pregnant and…you don't want any children. But I won't give up our baby." Her words were almost indistinguishable among her sobs. "I don't care how you feel, but I'm keeping this tiny part of you after our agreement is over."

Luke pulled her down to the carpet and cradled her in his arms.

"You're having my baby?"

"I know how you feel about being a father, about what your parent's did to you Luke, but this child will be something to remind me of you after our contract is over. I'll give it all the love it needs because it will remind me of how loving you can be."

He scooped Rhia up into his lap.

"I'll be damned if I divorce you!" He dabbed at her tear-drenched eyes. "I'm going to tell you something that will probably shock you. I love living at Greywood Hall and I've proved I can easily make it my main base. I'd definitely hate to bring up a child in this mausoleum, but I think Greywood is a perfect place for any children we'll have."

She still looked stunned…and doubtful.

"I was wrong to say I didn't want children because I really do want them with you. You're nothing like my mother."

"You do?"

"Will you marry me properly, Rhia Ashton?"

Rhia's smile was watery. She still sounded so tentative, not as enthusiastic as he'd hoped for.

"I can't go on with future plans without telling you what Meg has also said."

He knew if Meg had said something else then he needed to listen.

"Meg says your mother had a miscarriage…around four months after she and your father had got married."

"And?" Luke had a feeling what came next would be shocking.

"The foetus was about seven months old, a female child." Rhia's breath hitched before she continued. "I've now found a hospital reference to back this up."

"So you're thinking that my father got my mother pregnant and felt he had to marry her?"

That made their whole cold marriage a more realistic possibility.

"Yes," Rhia answered. "But that's not the most difficult thing to tell you. Meg was really at pains to tell me she honestly wasn't gossiping and that she doesn't ever want to hurt you."

"I had a feeling she had more to say. I've never ever seen Meg so disturbed." He smoothed his fingertips across Rhia's tense brow.

"Meg was distraught when she told me these things, Luke. She's hated to keep them secret for so long and she's desperate that you don't ever think badly of her."

"How can she ever think that," he cried, "she was always my rock."

Rhia's eyes sought his before she continued. "Meg's words were…'Elizabeth preferred the company of women.' It seems it wasn't possible for Meg not to know that some of your mother's female guests were also your mother's lovers."

"What?" Luke rolled Rhia off his thighs and shot up to his feet.

"I'm so sorry!" She followed and threw her arms around his waist. "I don't mean to hurt you, but it might explain why she didn't seem to love you, Luke."

"Good God! I really must have been a mistake then."

Rhia continued, stroking his back to calm him, "Meg thinks that your mother tried to sublimate her sexuality and forced herself into a relationship with a man – your father. It seems she got pregnant almost immediately. They got married but then Elizabeth miscarried. According to Meg they always had separate bedrooms, even right after the wedding, and she doesn't think they ever slept together again till around the months that they conceived you, again a time when Meg thinks your mother deliberately seduced your father into going along with her plan of trying for another child."

"So you're saying I wasn't quite a mistake?"

"I don't think so…" Rhia still sounded hesitant.

"Not a mistake then, but knowing my mother I was the thing that would have gained her credibility in Brisbane society. And having done her duty, she could then have affairs with women as much as she liked. What the hell did my father think of her plans?"

"Meg reckons that your father actually did love your mother at first, or at least the woman he thought she was. She thinks he eventually realised she couldn't love him as a woman should but wouldn't divorce her after your birth, since you were his legitimate son."

"And Italians didn't do divorce." His laugh was tense, and hurt.

"But he couldn't love me either?"

He watched the anguish flit across Rhia's face. "No. It seems he just couldn't quite manage to love you. Or at least he couldn't show it."

"And my mother?"

Rhia's face clouded. "Meg reckons if you'd been a girl, like her first baby, Elizabeth might have loved you – or at least liked you better."

A letter arrived from Amelia Greywood's lawyer the day after the year of cohabitation was completed, confirming that Greywood Hall had officially passed into his ownership. It was accompanied by another letter from Amelia herself, written after her latest will revisions, less than one year before her death. In it she explained that her expectation was that he would love living in a restored Greywood Hall with the woman of his dreams.

Snuggling down on the couch with Rhia in his arms, he read out the letter.

"I also apologise, Luke, for any serious inconvenience I may have caused you when you made your decision. I knew from my very clever private detective that your finances were in good shape. Perfectly sound enough for you to restore Greywood to the splendour it used to be. You were at liberty to walk away totally, of course, and leave Greywood to rot...but I truly hoped you wouldn't do that.

My greatest wish was that you didn't sell the property without having had the opportunity to experience the pleasures that could be had from it. I knew you'd had many women friends over the years but had not yet settled on one particular woman.

If you're reading this letter after the property is legally yours, I really do hope the woman you have married is the perfect woman that you want to be with for the rest of your life.

I have never been able to fill Greywood with my own spouse and children, but it would please me greatly to know that you will.'

He read on that in including the matrimony clause, Amelia's intention was merely meant to be a nudge in the direction of him settling down and staying in one place, specifically at her beloved Greywood. She also wrote that she couldn't ever countenance selling it because she couldn't bear to have it go completely out of the family connection, even though he was the one and only very remote link.

Amelia had finished the letter even more heartbreakingly.

"My sources had shown me that your parents' marriage was perhaps not particularly successful and I wept for the lonely boy that I know you must have been, Luke. But when you were younger it was not my place to

intervene. It was your mother who chose not to continue contact with me."

Rhia gasped at that before he read on.

"You may be surprised to know that I have met you once, when you were only weeks old, but your mother decided at that time that she didn't want any further communication with me. I think she was ashamed that Greywood Hall had sunk to such low depths and that the coffers were bare. She was also extremely upset when I informed her that her father had been born illegitimate, as was I myself. She wanted no-one to ever know about those social infringements.'

"Oh my God, Luke!" Rhia cried, "Poor Amelia. I think your mother must have hurt her very badly."

He paced around, the letter almost crumpled in his hand. "I know exactly how hurtful my mother would have been. She rarely minced her words and I'm sure Amelia would have had a virulent mouthful."

He gathered Rhia in his arms and rested their foreheads together, a place he always found comforting. "She was such a cold hearted bitch!"

A few moments later, they resumed their reading of the letter since Amelia wasn't quite done yet. She had written that she'd had irregular communication with her aunt Jocasta when she was in her twenties, her aunt having re-established the link. But she'd had virtually no communication with Alexander, who had wanted to sever all connections with his English heritage. Amelia had only had one hurtful letter from Alexander, who'd been made aware of the lack of money at Greywood Hall and had written back to her, one time only, saying that there was no way he was going to be shackled with a white elephant back in England.

Amelia had finished her letter with a heartfelt plea.

"Please forgive me for meddling in your life and accept my sincerest wishes for your future."

"Oh, Luke! That is so sad." Rhia cried on his shoulder and held him tight because she knew how affected he'd been by the last revelations in the mystery that was his legacy at Greywood.

On their flight back to England, he and Rhia made plans for the celebratory event she had briefly outlined to him so many months before.

Although it was short notice for such a spectacular event, Greywood Hall was already completed. All he had to do was make it happen – not such a problem really as Rhia, in her enthusiasm way back then, had already sketched out the planning details for a grand period-dress reception.

It took place one month after he became the official owner of Greywood Hall.

Rhia compromised on their new wedding by agreeing to a ceremony in the fabulously restored gardens at Greywood Hall, where he retook his vows in earnest. Rhia had also written her own, both reciting them a short time before the bulk of the guests arrived. Those attending the early ceremony were the most important of their friends and acquaintances. Much to his amusement Rhia had chosen to be given away by her friend Gus – though her father and family attended as important guests.

Rhia wore a frothy white confection that made her look like his nymph of the woods. They'd chosen it together just like he'd envisaged so many months before. It exactly matched his idea of what his bride should wear, albeit she was much fatter around the waist. Thor at Rhia's side was her only attendant. The dog was far too large a hound to wear any decorative touches, but it amused all present when Thor darted off to fetch him a stick which was promptly dropped at his feet.

When the throng departed, Luke whisked an exhausted Rhia back to their bedroom where he made a theatrical event out of removing her clothes. He kissed her soundly and declared, "I love everything about you."

She gurgled into his neck, "You liar. I'm a big fat flab now."

"Yes," he agreed, grinning like a Cheshire cat. "But you're my big fat flab. And with you by my side we'll put the life back into Greywood that Amelia craved."

"We both will, along with our children."

"Children?" His mumble backed Rhia carefully down onto the bed. "I like the sound of that. When can we start on number two?"

Other novels by Nancy Jardine

With Ocelot Press
Contemporary Fiction
Romantic Comedy Mystery *Take Me Now*
Romantic Mystery Thriller *Topaz Eyes*
Historical Fiction - *Celtic Fervour Series*
Book 1 *The Beltane Choice*
Book 2 *After Whorl: Bran Reborn*
Book 3 *After Whorl: Donning Double Cloaks*
Book 4 *Agricola's Bane*

Time Travel Historical Adventure
The Taexali Game

Buy Nancy Jardine's books from Amazon. Signed paperback versions available directly from the author (contact via email or website)

Email: nan_jar@btinternet.com
Website: http://www.nancyjardineauthor.com/
Blog: https://nancyjardine.blogspot.com
Twitter: @nansjar

Nominations

Topaz Eyes, was a Finalist for THE PEOPLE'S BOOK PRIZE FICTION 2014
After Whorl: Bran Reborn, Book 2 of the Celtic Fervour Series, was accepted for THE WALTER SCOTT PRIZE FOR HISTORICAL FICTION 2014.
The Taexali Game (time travel set in Roman 'Aberdeenshire' AD 210) 2nd Place Best Self Published Book in the SCOTTISH ASSOCIATION OF WRITERS Competition 2017 & *indieBRAG* Medallion, Jan 2018.
Celtic Fervour Series are Discovered Diamonds

Ocelot Press

Thank you for reading this Ocelot Press book. If you enjoyed it, we'd greatly appreciate it if you could take a moment to write a short review on the website where you bought the book (e.g. Amazon), and/or on Goodreads, or recommend it to a friend. Sharing your thoughts helps other readers to choose good books, and authors to keep writing.

You might like to try books by other Ocelot Press authors. We cover a range of genres, with a focus on historical fiction (including historical mystery and paranormal), romance and fantasy. To find out more, please don't hesitate to connect with us.

Website: https://ocelotpress.wordpress.com/
Email: ocelotpress@gmail.com
Twitter: @OcelotPress
Facebook: https://www.facebook.com/OcelotPress

Dear Reader,

Thank you for reading **Monogamy Twist.** I hope you enjoyed reading it as much as I loved creating it!

Posting your thoughts after reading *Monogamy Twist* on Amazon (or on the site the book was bought from) will help me with future mystery writing, and they'll be much appreciated. Alternatively please email me at *nan_jar@btinternet.com* Reader reviews and comments can help me gain more visibility across the internet and, in turn, they help to increase readership and sales. Sometimes ideas occur to a reader that the author may not have thought about but which are good to include in new editions.

A review is also very useful for potential new readers to decide if it's a book they might like to buy and add to their reading pile.

Wishing you fun with future reading!

Nancy Jardine